THE BLOW CAME SUDDENLY ...

Carella knew it wasn't a fist. He knew it was something long and hard as it struck him across his eyes and the bridge of his nose and sent him stumbling back against the hedge. As he tried to reach for his revolver, another blow came. There was a soft whistling sound on the early night air, the sound of a rapier, or a stick, or a baseball bat. This time the blow struck him on his right shoulder, hard. His gun dropped to the ground. The end of the unseen weapon gouged into his stomach like a battering ram, and then the sharp edge was striking his face again, repeatedly, numbingly. He lashed out at the darkness with his left hand, but there was blood in his eyes, a terrible pain in his nose, and a world of nothingness ready to embrace him forever. . . .

SIGNET Mysteries You'll Enjoy

Like Love

An 87th Precinct Mystery

by Ed McBain

Ⓞ
A SIGNET BOOK

NEW AMERICAN LIBRARY

Library of Congress Catalog Card Number: 62-19078

Published by arrangement with Ed McBain

SIGNET, SIGNET CLASSIC, MENTOR, PLUME, MERIDIAN AND NAL
BOOKS *are published by New American Library,*
1633 Broadway, New York, New York 10019

FIRST SIGNET PRINTING, NOVEMBER, 1976

5   6   7   8   9   10   11   12   13

This is for
Vivian and Jack Farren

The city in these pages is imaginary.
The people, the places, are all fictitious.
Only the police routine is based
on established investigatory technique.

1

The woman on the ledge was wearing a nightgown. It was only three-thirty in the afternoon, but she was dressed for sleep, and the brisk spring breezes flattened the sheer nylon fabric against her body so that she looked like a legendary Greek figure sculptured in stone, immobile, on the ledge twelve stories above the city street.

The police and the fire department had gone through the whole bit—they had seen this particular little drama a thousand times in the movies and on television. If there was anything that bored civil service employees, it was a real-life enactment of an entertainment cliché. So the firemen spread their nets in the street below, and got their loudspeakers going, and the policemen roped off the block and sent a couple of detectives up to the window where spring flattened the girl against the brick wall of the building.

She was a pretty girl, a young girl in her early twenties, with long blond hair caught by the April breeze and whipped furiously about her face and head. Andy Parker, one of the sweet-talkers sent over by the 87th Squad was wishing the girl would come in off the ledge so he could get a closer look at the full breasts beneath the sheer nightgown. Steve Carella, the other detective, simply didn't think anyone should die on such a nice spring day.

The girl didn't seem to know either of the detectives was there. She had moved away from the window through which she had gained access to the ledge, had gingerly inched her way toward the corner of the building and stood there now with her arms behind her and her fingers spread for a grip on the rust-red wall of the building. The ledge was perhaps a foot wide, running around the twelfth floor, broken at the building's corner by one of those grotesque gargoyles which adorned many of the city's older structures. The girl was unaware of the grinning stone head, unaware of the detectives who leaned out of the window some six feet away from her. She stared straight ahead of her, the long blond hair whipping over her shoulders in a bright gold tangle against the red brick of the wall. Occasionally, she looked

1

down to the street below. There was no emotion on her face. There was no conviction, no determination, no fear. Her face was a beautiful blank washed clean by the wind; her body a voluptuous, thinly sheathed, wind-caressed part of the building.

"Miss?" Carella said.

She did not turn toward him. Her eyes stared straight ahead of her.

"Miss?"

Again, she did not acknowledge his presence. She looked down into the street instead and then, suddenly remembering she was a good-looking woman, suddenly remembering that hundreds of eyes were fixed upon her nearly naked figure, she moved one arm across her breasts, as if to protect herself. She almost lost her balance. She tottered for an instant, and then her hand moved quickly from the front of the gown, touched the rust-red brick again in reassurance. Carella, watching her, suddenly knew she did not plan to die.

"Can you hear me, miss?" Carella said.

"I can hear you," she answered without turning toward him. "Go away." Her voice was toneless.

"Well, I'd like to, but I can't." He waited for an answer, but none came. "I'm supposed to stay here until you come off that ledge."

The girl nodded once, briefly. Without turning, she said, "Go home. You're wasting your time."

"I couldn't go home in any case," Carella said. "I don't get relieved until five forty-five." He paused. "What time do you think it is now?"

"I don't have a watch," the girl said.

"Well, what time do you think it is?"

"I don't know what time it is, and I don't care. Look, I know what you're trying to do. You're trying to get me in conversation. I don't want to talk to you. Go away."

"Listen, I don't want to talk to you either," Carella said. "But the lieutenant said 'Go over and talk to that nut on the ledge.' So here I . . ."

"I'm not a nut!" the girl said vehemently, turning to Carella for the first time.

"Listen, *I* didn't say it, the lieutenant did."

"Yeah, well you go back and tell your lieutenant to go straight to hell."

"Why don't you come back with me and tell him yourself?"

The girl did not answer. She turned from him again and

2

looked down into the street. It seemed she would jump in that moment. Quickly, Carella said, "What's your name?"

"I don't have any name."

"Everybody has a name."

"My name is Catherine the Great."

"Come on."

"It's Marie Antoinette. It's Cleopatra. I'm a nut, isn't that what you said? All right, I'm a nut, and that's my name."

"Which one?"

"Any one you like. Or all of them. Go away, will you?"

"I'll bet your name is Blanche," Carella said.

"Who told you that?"

"Your landlady."

"What else did she tell you?"

"That your name is Blanche Mattfield, that you come from Kansas City, and that you've been living here for six months. Is that right?"

"Go ask *her*, that nosy bitch."

"Well, *is* your name Blanche?"

"Yes, my name is Blanche. Oh, for God's sake, do we have to go through this? I can see *clear* through you, mister. You're made of glass. Will you please go away and leave me in peace?"

"To do what? To jump down into the street?"

"Yes, that's right. That's exactly right. To jump down into the street."

"Why?"

The girl did not answer.

"Aren't you a little chilly out there?" Carella asked.

"No."

"That's a strong wind."

"I don't feel it."

"Shall I get you a sweater?"

"No."

"Why don't you come in off there, Blanche? Come on. You're gonna catch cold out there."

The girl laughed suddenly and startlingly. Carella, unaware that he had said anything funny, was surprised by the outburst.

"*I'm* ready to kill myself," the girl said, "and *you're* worried about my catching cold."

"I'd say the chances of your catching cold are better than the chances of your killing yourself," Carella said softly.

"You would, huh?"

"I would," Carella said.

3

"Mmm-huh," the girl said.

"That's right."

"Then you're going to be in for a hell of a surprise."

"Am I?" Carella asked.

"I can guarantee it."

"You're pretty set on killing yourself, huh, Blanche?"

"Really, *must* I listen to this?" she said. "Won't you please, please go away?"

"No. I don't think you want to die. I'm afraid you'll fall off that ledge and hurt yourself and some of the people down below, too."

"I want to die," the girl said softly.

"Why?"

"You really want to know why?"

"Yes. I'd really like to know."

"Because," she said slowly and clearly, "I am lonely, and unloved, and unwanted." She nodded, and then turned her head because her eyes had suddenly flooded with tears, and she did not want Carella to see them.

"A pretty girl like you, huh? Lonely, and unloved, and unwanted. How old are you, Blanche?"

"Twenty-two."

"And you never want to get to be twenty-three, huh?"

"I never want to get to be twenty-three," she repeated tonelessly. "I don't want to get another minute older, not another second older. I want to die. Won't you please leave me alone to die?"

"Stop it, stop it," Carella said chidingly. "I don't like to hear that kind of talk. Dying, dying, you're twenty-two years old! You've got your whole life ahead of you."

"Nothing," she said.

"*Every*thing!"

"Nothing. He's gone, there's nothing, he's gone."

"Who?"

"Nobody. Everybody. Oh! Oh!" She put one hand to her face suddenly and began weeping into it. With the other hand, she clung to the building, swaying. Carella leaned further out of the window, and she turned to him sharply and shouted, "Don't come near me!"

"I wasn't . . ."

"Don't come out here!"

"Look, take it easy. I wouldn't come out there if you gave me a million dollars."

"All right. Stay where you are. If you come near me, I'll jump."

4

"Yeah, and who's gonna care if you do, Blanche?"

"What?"

"If you jump, if you die, you think anyone'll care?"

"No, I . . . I know that. No one'll care. I . . . I'm not worried about that."

"You'll be a two-line blurb on page four, and then nothing. Nothing lasts a long time."

"I don't care. Oh, please, won't you please leave me alone? Can't you understand?"

"No, I can't. I wish you'd explain it to me."

The girl swallowed and nodded, and then turned to him and slowly and patiently said, "He's gone, do you see?"

"Who's gone?"

"Does it matter? He. A man. And he's gone. Goodbye, Blanche, it's been fun. That's all. Fun. And I . . ." Her eyes suddenly flared. "Damn you, I don't want to live! I don't want to live without him!"

"There are other men."

"No." She shook her head. "No. I loved him. I love him. I don't want any other men. I want . . ."

"Come on in," Carella said. "We'll have a cup of coffee, and we'll try to . . ."

"No."

"Come on, come on. You're not going to jump off that damn ledge. You're just wasting everybody's time. Now, come on."

"I'm going to jump."

"Sure, but not right now, huh? Some other time. Next week maybe, next year. But we're very busy today. The kids are turning on fire hydrants all over the city. Spring is here, Blanche. Do me a favor and jump some other time, okay?"

"Go to hell," she said, and then looked down to the street.

"Blanche?"

She did not answer.

"Blanche?" Carella sighed and turned to Parker. He whispered something in Parker's ear, and Parker nodded and left the window.

"You remind me a little of my wife," Carella said to the girl. She did not answer. "Really, my wife. Teddy. She's a deaf-mute. She . . ."

"A what?"

"A mute. Born deaf and dumb." Carella smiled. "You think you've got problems? How'd you like to be deaf and dumb and married to a cop besides?"

"Is she really . . . deaf and dumb?"

5

"Sure."

"I'm sorry."

"Don't be. She never even *thinks* of throwing herself off a building."

"I . . . I wasn't going to do it this way," the girl said. "I was going to take sleeping pills. That's why I put on the nightgown. But . . . I wasn't sure I had enough. I had only half a bottle. Would that have been enough?"

"Enough to make you sick," Carella said. "Come on in, Blanche. I'll tell you all about the time I almost slashed my wrists."

"You never did."

"I almost did, I swear to God. Look, everybody feels like hell every once in a while. What happened? Did you get your period today?"

"Wh . . . ? How . . . how did you know?"

"I figured. Come on."

"No."

"Come on, Blanche."

"No! Stay away from me!"

From inside the apartment, there came the sudden shrill ring of a telephone. The sound was clearly heard by the girl. She turned her head for a moment, and then closed her mind to the ringing phone. Carella pretended surprise. He had sent Parker downstairs to call the girl's number, but now he pretended the ringing was unexpected. Quietly, he said, "Your phone's ringing."

"I'm not home."

"It might be important."

"It isn't."

"It might be . . . him."

"He's in California. It's not him. I don't care who it is." She paused. Again, she said, "He's in California."

"They have phones in California, you know," Carella said.

"It's . . . it's not him."

"Why don't you answer it and find out?"

"I *know* it isn't him! Leave me alone!"

"You want us to answer this?" someone in the apartment shouted.

"She's coming," Carella said. He extended his hand to the girl. The telephone kept ringing behind him. "Take my hand, Blanche," he said.

"No. I'm going to jump."

"You're not going to jump. You're going to come inside and answer your telephone."

6

"No! I said no!"

"Come on, you're getting me sore," Carella shouted. "Are you just a stupid broad, is that what you are? You want to squash your brains on that sidewalk? It's made of cement, Blanche! That's not a mattress down there."

"I don't care. I'm going to jump."

"So jump, for Christ's sake!" Carella said angrily, using the tone of a father whose patience has finally been exhausted. "If you're going to jump, go ahead. Then we can all go home. Go ahead."

"I will," she said.

"So go ahead. Either jump, or take my hand. We're wasting time here."

Behind him, the phone kept ringing furiously. There was no sound in the apartment, no sound on the face of the building except for the ringing of the telephone and the sighing of the wind.

"I will," the girl said softly.

"Here," Carella said. "Here's my hand. Take it."

For a speechless, shocking moment, he didn't realize quite what was happening. And then his eyes opened wide, and he stood stock-still at the window, his hand extended, his hand frozen in space as the girl suddenly shoved herself away from the wall and leaped.

He heard her scream, heard it trailing all the way down the twelve stories to the street below, drowning out the frenzied ringing of the telephone. And then he heard the sound of her body striking the pavement, and he turned blindly from the window and said to no one, "Jesus, she did it."

The salesman was going to be a dead man within the next five minutes.

Some twenty blocks away from where Blanche leaped to her death, he entered a street flirting with Spring, carrying a heavy sample case in one hand, and attributing gender to the vernal equinox. To the salesman, Spring was a woman who had come dancing in over the River Harb, flitting past flotsam and jetsam, those two old-time vaudeville performers, showing her legs to the passing, hooting tugs, winking lewdly at the condoms floating on the river's edge, flashing fleshy thighs to Silvermine Road and the park, and then airily leaping over the tenement rooftops to land gracefully in the middle of the street. The people had come outdoors to greet her. They wore smiles and flowered house dresses, smiles and open-throat sports shirts, smiles and sneakers and T shirts and shorts. Grin-

7

ning, they took Spring into their arms and held her close and kissed her throat, where you been all this time, baby?

The salesman didn't know he was going to be a dead man, of course. If he'd known, he probably wouldn't have been spending his last few minutes on earth carrying a heavy sample case full of hairbrushes down a city street making love to Spring. If he'd known he was about to die, he might have saluted or something. Or, at the very least, he might have thrown his sample case into the air and gone to Bora Bora. Ever since he'd read *Hawaii*, he had gone to Bora Bora often. Sometimes, when selling hairbrushes got particularly rough, he went to Bora Bora as often as ten or twelve times a day. Once he got to Bora Bora, he made love to dusky-skinned fifteen-year-old maidens. There were a few dusky-skinned fifteen-year-old maidens on the street today, but not very many. Besides, he didn't know he was going to die.

He came down the street heavily, feeling like Lee J. Cobb minus one sample case. He wondered whether he'd sell any more brushes today; he needed three more sales before he filled his quota, who the hell wanted to buy hairbrushes when Spring was holding a dance in the street? Sighing, he climbed the stoop of the nearest tenement, passing a pimply-faced sixteen-year-old blond girl wearing dungarees and a white blouse, and wondering whether she knew how to hula. He entered the dim and foul-smelling vestibule, walking past the mailboxes with their broken locks and hanging front flaps, and then past the open and miraculously intact frosted-glass inner door. Garbage cans were stacked alongside the staircase wall on the ground floor. They were empty, but their stench permeated the hallway. He sniffed in discomfort, and then began climbing the steps toward the natural light coming from the air-shaft window on the first floor.

He had three minutes to live.

The sample case was heavier when you climbed. The more you climbed, the heavier it got. He had noticed that. He was a particularly astute human being, he felt, intelligent and observant, and he had noticed over the years that there was a direct correlation between the physical act of climbing and the steadily increasing weight of his sample case during the ascent. He was pleased when he gained the first-floor landing. He put the sample case down, reached for his handkerchief, and mopped his brow.

He had a minute and a half to live.

He folded the handkerchief carefully and put it back into his pocket. He looked up at the metal numerals on the door

8

ahead of him. Apartment 1A. The A was hanging slightly askew. Time was running out.

He located the bell button set into the door jamb.

He reached out with his forefinger.

Three seconds.

He touched the button.

The sudden blinding explosion ripped away the front wall of the apartment, tore the salesman in half, and sent a cascade of hairbrushes and burnt human flesh roaring into the air and down the stairwell.

Spring was really here.

2

Detective 2nd/Grade Cotton Hawes had served aboard a P.T. boat during the last great war for democracy, and his battle experience had therefore been limited to sea engagements alone. He had, to be fair, once participated in the shore bombardment of a tiny Pacific island, but he had never seen the results of his vessel's devastating torpedo attack on a Japanese dock installation. Had he been a foot soldier in Italy, the chaos in the tenement hallway would not have surprised him very much. But he had had a clean bed to sleep in, and three squares a day, as the saying goes, and so the ruin confronting him just inside the vestibule door was something of a shock.

The hallway and the staircase were littered with plaster, lath, wallpaper, wooden beams, kitchen utensils, hairbrushes, broken crockery, human flesh, blood, hair, and garbage. A cloud of settling plaster dust hovered in the air, pierced by the afternoon sunlight which slanted through the air-shaft window. The window itself had been shattered by the explosion, a skeleton of its former self, with broken glass shards covering the first-floor landing. The walls surrounding the window and the staircase were blackened and blistered. Every milk bottle resting in the hallway outside the other two apartments on the landing had been shattered by the blast. Fortunately, the seductress Spring had lured the other first-floor tenants into the street, and so the only loss of human life that April afternoon had been in the hallway and in apartment 1A itself.

Following a coughing, choking patrolman up the littered staircase, Hawes covered his face with a handkerchief and tried not to realize he was climbing past the blood-soaked squishy remains of what had once been a human being. He followed a trail of hairbrushes to the shattered wall and demolished doorway of the apartment; it had rained hairbrushes that day, it had rained hairbrushes and blood. He entered the apartment. Smoke still billowed from the kitchen, and there was the unmistakable aroma of gas in the air. Hawes had not thought he would need the mask which had been pressed into

10

his hand by the patrolman downstairs, but one whiff of the stench changed his mind. He pulled the face piece over his head, checked the inlet tube connected to the cannister, and followed the patrolman into the kitchen, cursing the fact that the glass eyeholes on the mask were beginning to fog up. A man in over-alls was busily working in the kitchen behind the demolished stove, trying to cut off the steady leakage of illuminating gas into the apartment. The explosion had ripped the stove from the wall, severing its connection with the pipes leading to the main, and the new steady flow of gas into the apartment threatened a build-up which could lead to a second explosion. The man in over-alls—undoubtedly sent by either the Department of Public Works or the Gas and Electric Company—didn't even look up when Hawes and the patrolman entered the room. He worked busily and quickly. There had been one explosion, and he damn well didn't want another, not while he was on the premises. He knew that a mixture of one part carbon monoxide to one-half part of oxygen, or two-and-a-half parts air was enough to cause an explosion in the presence of a flame or a spark. He had opened every window in the joint when he'd arrived—even the one in the bedroom where what was on the bed didn't particularly appeal to his esthetic sense. He had then gone immediately to work on the bent and twisted pipes, trying to stop the flow of gas. He was a devout Catholic, but even if the Pope himself had walked into that kitchen, he would not have stopped work on the pipes. Hawes and the patrolman didn't even rate a nod.

Through the fogged eyepieces of his mask, Hawes watched the man working on the pipes and then glanced around the demolished kitchen. It did not take a mastermind to determine that this was the room where the explosion had taken place. Even without the presence of the up-ended stove and the stench of illuminating gas, the room itself was a shambles—it had to be the nucleus of the blast. Every pane of glass had been shattered, every pot and pan hurled through the air and peppered with holes. The curtains had gone up in instant flame—happily, there had not been a major conflagration. The table and chairs had been tossed into the room closest to the kitchen, and even in that room, the sofa had been blasted out of place and rested up-ended against one damaged wall.

The bedroom, in contrast to the other two rooms, had been almost untouched. The window had been opened by the gasman, and the spring breeze touched the curtains, played idly with them. The blanket had been drawn back to the foot of the bed. There were two people lying on the clean white bed-

11

sheet. One was a man, the other was a woman; that's the way it is in the spring. The man was wearing undershorts and nothing else. The undershorts were striped in blue. The woman was wearing only her panties.

They were both dead.

Hawes did not know very much about pathology, but the man and woman on the bed—even when viewed through his fogging mask—were both a bright cherry-red color; and he was willing to bet his shield they had died of acute carbon monoxide poisoning. He was further willing to speculate that the death was either accidental or suicidal. He was too good a cop to rule out homicide immediately, but he nonetheless began a methodical search for a suicide note.

He did not have to look very far.

The note was on the dresser opposite the bed. It had been placed flat on the dresser top, and then a man's wrist watch had been put on top of it to hold it down. Without touching either the wrist watch or the note, Hawes bent over to read what had been written.

The note had been typed. He automatically glanced around the room to see if he could locate the machine and saw it resting on a small end table near the bed. He turned his attention back to the note.

```
Dear God, forgive us for this terrible thing.
We are so much in love, and the world is all
against us. There is no other way. Now we can
end the suffering of ourselfs and others. Please
understand.

                              Tommy and Irene
```

Hawes nodded once, in silent understanding, and then made a memo to pick up both note and wrist watch as soon as the photographers were finished with the room. He walked across the room and filled out a tag which he would later affix to the typewriter for delivery to the laboratory where Lieutenant Sam Grossman's boys would perform their comparison tests.

He walked back to the bed.

The man and woman appeared to be in their early twenties. The man had involuntarily soiled himself, probably after sinking into a deep coma once the gas had really taken hold. The woman had vomited into her pillow. He stood at

12

the foot of the bed and wondered what they had thought it would be like. A nice quiet peaceful death? Something like going to sleep? He wondered how they had felt when the headache appeared and they began to get drowsy and faint and unable to move themselves off that bed even if they'd changed their minds about dying together. He wondered how they'd felt just when their bodies had begun to twitch, just before they passed into a stupor where vomiting and evacuation were things beyond their control. He looked at this dead man and woman in their early twenties—Tommy and Irene—and he shook his head and thought, *You poor stupid boobs, what did you hope to find? What made you think a painful death was the answer to a painful life?*

He turned his eyes away from the bed.

Two empty whisky bottles were on the floor. One of them had spilled alcohol onto the scatter rug on the woman's side of the bed. He didn't know whether or not they had drunk themselves into insensibility after turning on the gas jet, but that seemed to be a standard part of the gas-pipe routine. He knew there were people who felt that suicide was an act of extreme bravery, but he could never look upon it as anything but utter cowardice. The empty whisky bottles gave conviction to his thoughts. He made out the tags for each bottle, again postponing the actual tagging until photographs had been made.

The woman's clothes were hung over the back and resting on the seat of a straight-backed chair alongside the bed. Her blouse was hanging, and her brassière was folded over it; her skirt, garter belt, nylons, and leather belt were folded on the seat. A pair of high-heeled black leather pumps were neatly placed at the foot of the chair.

The man's clothes were over and on an easy chair at the other end of the room. Trousers, shirt, undershirt, tie, socks, and belt. His shoes were placed to one side of the chair. Hawes made a note to have the technicians pick up the clothing, which they would place in plastic bags for transmission to the laboratory. He also noted the man's wallet, tie clip, and loose change lying on the dresser top, together with the woman's earrings and an imitation pearl necklace.

By the time he'd finished his search of the apartment, the gas leak had been plugged, the laboratory boys, police photographers, and assistant medical examiner had arrived, and there was nothing to do but go downstairs again and talk to the patrolman who had reported the explosion to the precinct. The patrolman was new and green and terrified. But he had

13

managed to pull his wits together long enough to find a charred and tattered wallet in the hallway rubble, and he turned this over to Hawes as if he were very anxious to get rid of it. Hawes almost wished the patrolman hadn't found it. The wallet gave an identity to the remains of a human being that had been spattered down the staircase and over the walls.

He called on the salesman's wife later that day, after he had spoken to the lab. The salesman's wife said, "Why did it have to be Harry?"

He explained that the lab's supposition was that her husband had probably approached the door of apartment 1A and pressed the buzzer and this in turn had caused an electrical spark which had precipitated the explosion.

"Why did it have to be Harry?" the salesman's wife asked.

Hawes tried to explain that these things happened sometimes, that they were nobody's fault, that her husband was simply doing his job and had no idea the apartment behind that door was full of illuminating gas. But the woman only stared at him blankly and said again, "Why did it have to be Harry?"

He went back to the squadroom with a weary ache inside him. He barely said hello to Carella who was at his own desk typing up a report. Both men left the squadroom at eight-fifteen that night, two-and-a-half hours after they were officially relieved. Carella was in a rotten mood. He ate a cold supper, snapped viciously at his wife, didn't even go in to peek at the sleeping twins, and went straight to bed where he tossed restlessly all night long. Hawes called Christine Maxwell, a girl he had known for a long time, and asked her to go to a movie with him. He watched the screen with interesting annoyance because something was bugging him about that apparent suicide and he couldn't quite figure out what.

3

Dead people do not sweat.

It was very warm in the morgue, and a light sheen of perspiration covered the faces of Carella and Hawes, clung to the upper lip of the man with them, stained the armpits of the attendant who looked at the three men bleakly for a moment and then pulled out the drawer.

The drawer moved almost soundlessly on its rollers. The girl Irene lay naked and dead on the slab; they had found her in her panties, but these had been shipped immediately to the lab, and she lay naked and cool and unsweating while the attendant and the three men looked down at her. In a little while, she would be shipped to another part of the hospital, where an autopsy would be performed. For now, her body was intact. All it lacked was life.

"Is that her?" Carella asked.

The man standing between the two detectives nodded. He was a tall, thin man with pale blue eyes and blond hair. He wore a gray gabardine suit, and a white button-down shirt with a striped tie. He did not say anything. He simply nodded, and even the nod was a brief one, as if motion were an extravagance.

"And she's your wife, sir?" Hawes asked.

The man nodded again.

"Could you give us her full name, sir?"

"Irene," the man said.

"Middle name?"

"That *is* her middle name."

"What do you mean?"

"Her name is Margaret Irene Thayer." The man paused. "She didn't like the name Margaret, so she used her middle name."

"She called herself Irene, is that right?"

"That's right."

"And your address, Mr. Thayer?"

"1134 Bailey Avenue."

"You were living there with your wife?"

"Yes."

Carella and Hawes glanced at each other. Homicide at its best stinks to high heaven because everyone walking this earth has a closet he'd prefer leaving closed and homicide rarely knocks before entering. The girl Margaret Irene Thayer had been found on a bed wearing only her panties, and she'd been lying alongside a man in his undershorts. The man who had just positively identified her was named Michael Thayer, and he was her husband, and one of those little closets had just been opened, and everyone was staring into it. Carella cleared his throat.

"Were . . . er . . . you and your wife separated, or . . . ?"

"No," Thayer said.

"I see," Carella answered. He paused again. "You know, Mr. Thayer, that . . . that your wife was found with a man."

"Yes. Their pictures were in the paper. That's why I called the police. I mean, when I saw Irene's picture in the paper. I figured it was some kind of mistake. Because I thought . . . you see, she'd told me she was going out to visit her mother and I never suspected . . . so you see, I thought it was a mistake. She was supposed to be spending the night at her mother's, you see. So I called her mother, and her mother said no, Irene hadn't been there, and then I thought . . . I don't know what I thought. So I called the police and asked if I could . . . could see . . . could see the body of the girl they'd . . . found."

"And this *is* your wife, Mr. Thayer? You have no doubts about that?"

"She . . . she's my wife," Thayer said.

"Mr. Thayer, you said you saw pictures of both your wife and the man in the newspa . . ."

"Yes."

"Did you happen to recognize the man?"

"No." Thayer paused. "Is . . . is he here, too?"

"Yes, sir."

"I want to see him."

"If you didn't recognize him, there's no need to . . ."

"I want to see him," Thayer repeated.

Carella shrugged and then nodded at the attendant. They followed him across the long, high-ceilinged room. Their footsteps echoed across the tiled floor. The attendant consulted a typewritten list on a clipboard, moved down the aisle, stooped, and pulled open a second drawer. Thayer stared down into the face of the man they'd found with his wife.

"He's dead," he said, but the words did not seem intended for anyone.

16

"Yes," Carella said.

Thayer nodded. He nodded again. "I want to keep looking at him. That's strange, isn't it? I want to find out what was so . . . *different* about him."

"You still don't recognize him?" Hawes asked.

"No. Who is he?"

"We don't know. There was no driver's license or other identification in his wallet. But one of the names on the suicide note was Tommy. Did your wife ever mention anyone named Tommy?"

"No."

"And you've never seen him before?"

"Never." Thayer paused. "There's something I don't understand. The apartment. Where . . . where you found them. Wasn't . . . couldn't you ask the landlady? Wouldn't she know his name?"

"She might. But that wasn't Tommy's apartment."

"What do you mean?"

"The landlady told us that apartment was rented by a man named Fred Hassler."

"Well, perhaps he was using another name," Thayer suggested.

Carella shook his head. "No. We brought the landlady down here for a look. This isn't Fred Hassler." He nodded to the attendant, and the attendant shoved the drawer back into place. "We're trying to locate Hassler now, but so far we haven't had any luck." Carella paused. He wiped his forehead and then said, "Mr. Thayer, if it's all right with you, we'd like to get out of here. There are some questions we have to ask you, but we'd prefer doing it over a cup of coffee, if that's all right with you."

"Yes, of course," Thayer said.

"You need me any more?" the attendant asked.

"No. Thanks a lot, Charlie."

"Yeah," Charlie said, and went back to reading *Playboy*.

They found a diner three blocks from the hospital, and they sat in a seat near the window and watched the girls going by outside in their thin spring cottons. Carella and Thayer ordered coffee. Hawes was a tea drinker. They sat sipping from hot mugs and listening to the whir of the overhead fans. It was spring, and the pretty girls were passing by outside, and no one wanted to discuss treachery and sudden death. But there had been sudden death, and the wife of Michael Thayer had been revealed by death in a compromis-

17

ing and apparently treacherous attitude, and so the questions had to be asked.

"You said your wife told you she was going to spend the night with her mother, is that right, Mr. Thayer?"

"Yes."

"What's her mother's name?"

"Mary Tomlinson. My wife's maiden name was Margaret Irene Tomlinson."

"Where does your mother-in-law live, Mr. Thayer?"

"Out on Sands Spit."

"Did your wife visit her frequently?"

"Yes."

"How often, Mr. Thayer?"

"At least once every two weeks. Sometimes more often."

"Alone, Mr. Thayer?"

"What?"

"Alone? Without you?"

"Yes. My mother-in-law and I don't get along."

"So you don't visit her, is that right?"

"That's right."

"But you did call her this morning after you saw Irene's picture in the paper."

"Yes. I called her."

"Then you do speak to her."

"I speak to her, but we don't get along. I told Irene if she wanted to go see her mother, she'd have to do it without me. That's all."

"Which is what she did," Hawes said, "on the average of once every two weeks, sometimes more often."

"Yes."

"And yesterday she told you she was going to her mother's and would spend the night there?"

"Yes."

"Did she often spend the night at her mother's?"

"Yes. Her mother is a widow, you see, and Irene felt she was alone and so she spent . . ." Thayer hesitated. He sipped at his coffee, put down his cup, and then looked up. "Well, now . . . now I don't know. I just don't know."

"What is it you don't know, Mr. Thayer?"

"Well, I used to think . . . well, the woman *is* alone, you know, and even if I don't like her, I didn't think I should stop her daughter from spending time with her. Irene, I mean."

"Yes."

"But now . . . after . . . after what's happened, I just don't know. I mean, I don't know whether Irene really spent

18

all that time with her mother or if . . . if . . . if . . ."
Thayer shook his head. Quickly, he picked up his coffee cup and gulped at the steaming liquid.

"Or if she spent it with this Tommy," Carella said.

Thayer nodded.

"What time did she leave the house yesterday, Mr. Thayer?" Hawes asked.

"I don't know. I went to work at eight. She was still there when I left."

"What sort of work do you do?"

"I write greeting-card verse."

"Free lance, or for some company?"

"Free lance."

"But you said you left the house yesterday to go to work. Does that mean you don't work at home?"

"That's right," Thayer said. "I have a little office downtown."

"Downtown where?"

"In the Brio Building. It's just a small office. A desk, a typewriter, a filing cabinet, and a couple of chairs. That's all I need."

"Do you go to that office every morning at eight?" Hawes asked.

"Yes. Except on weekends. I don't usually work on weekends. Once in a while, but not usually."

"But Monday to Friday, you get to your office at eight in the morning, is that right?"

"I don't *get* there at eight. I leave my house at eight. I stop for breakfast, and *then* I go to my office."

"What time do you get there?"

"About nine."

"And what time do you quit?"

"About four."

"And then do you go straight home?" Carella asked.

"No. I usually stop for a drink with the man who has the office across the hall. He's a song writer. There's a lot of song writers in the Brio Building."

"What's his name?"

"Howard Levin."

"Did you go for a drink with him yesterday afternoon?"

"Yes."

"At four o'clock?"

"Around that time. I guess it was closer to four-thirty."

"May I give a recap on this, Mr. Thayer?" Hawes asked.

"Yesterday, you left your home at eight o'clock in the morning, went for breakfast . . ."

"Where was that?" Carella asked.

"I eat at the R and N Restaurant. That's two blocks from my house."

"You ate breakfast at the R and N," Hawes said, "and arrived at your office in the Brio Building at nine o'clock. Your wife was still at home when you left, but you knew she was going out to visit her mother on Sands Spit, or at least that's what she had told you."

"Yes, that's right."

"Did you talk to your wife at any time during the day?"

"No," Thayer said.

"Is there a telephone in your office?"

"Yes, of course." Thayer frowned. Something seemed to be bothering him all at once. He did not say what it was, not immediately, but his brows lowered, and his mouth hardened.

"But you didn't call her, nor did she call you."

"No," Thayer said, his voice taking on a curiously defensive tone. "I knew she was going to her mother's. Why would I call her?"

"What time did you go to lunch, Mr. Thayer?" Carella asked.

"One o'clock. I think it was one, anyway. Around that time. What is this?" he said suddenly.

"What is *what*, Mr. Thayer?"

"Never mind."

"Where'd you have lunch?" Hawes asked.

"At an Italian restaurant near the office."

"The name?"

"Look . . ." Thayer started, and then shook his head.

"Yes?"

"What is this?"

"Mr. Thayer," Hawes said flatly, "your wife was playing around with another man. It looks as if they committed suicide together, but a lot of things aren't always what they look like."

"I see."

"So we want to make sure . . ."

"I see," Thayer said again. "You think I had something to do with it, is that it?"

"Not necessarily," Carella said. "We're simply trying to find out how and where you spent your time yesterday."

"I see."

The table went silent.

"Where *did* you have lunch, Mr. Thayer?"

"Am I under arrest?" Thayer asked.

"No, sir."

"I have a feeling you can get me in trouble," Thayer said. "I don't think I want to answer any more questions."

"Why not?"

"Because I had nothing to do with this thing, and you're trying to make it sound as if . . . as if . . . goddammit, how do you think I feel?" he shouted suddenly. "I see my wife's picture in the paper, and the story tells me she's dead and . . . and . . . and was was was . . . you lousy bastards, how do you think I feel?"

He put down his coffee cup and covered his face with one hand. They could not tell whether or not he was crying behind that hand. He sat silent and said nothing.

"Mr. Thayer," Carella said gently, "our department investigates every suicide exactly the way it would a homicide. The same people are notified, the same reports are . . ."

"The hell with you *and* your department," Thayer said from behind his hand. "My wife is dead."

"Yes, sir, we realize that."

"Then leave me alone, can't you? I thought . . . you said we would have a cup of coffee and . . . now it's . . . this is a third degree."

"No, sir, it's not a third degree."

"Then what the hell is it?" Thayer said. His hand suddenly dropped from his face. His eyes flashed. "My wife is *dead!*" he shouted. "She was in bed with another man! What the hell is it you want from me?"

"We want to know where you were all day yesterday," Hawes said. "That's all."

"I went to lunch at a restaurant called Nino's. It's on the Stem, two blocks from my office. I got back to the office at about two or two-thirty. I worked until . . ."

"Did you have lunch alone?"

"No. Howard was with me."

"Go on."

"I worked until about four-thirty. Howard came in and said he was knocking off, and would I like a drink. I said yes I would. We went to the bar on the corner, it's called Dinty's. I had two Rob Roys, and then Howard and I walked to the subway. I went straight home."

"What time was that?"

"About five-thirty."

"Then what?"

"I read the papers and I watched the news on television,

21

and then I made myself some bacon and eggs and then I got into my pajamas and read a while, and then I went to bed. I got up at seven-thirty this morning. I left the house at eight. I bought a paper on the way to the R and N. While I was having breakfast, I saw Irene's picture. I called my mother-in-law from the restaurant, and then I called the police." Thayer paused. Sarcastically, he added, "They were kind enough to provide me with you two gentlemen."

"Okay, Mr. Thayer," Hawes said.

"Is that all?"

"That's all. I'm sorry we upset you, but there are questions we have to ask and . . ."

"May I go now?"

"Yes, sir."

"Thank you." Thayer paused. "Would you do me a favor?"

"What's that?"

"When you find out who the man was . . . Tommy, the man she was in . . . in bed with . . . would you let me know?"

"If you want us to."

"Yes, I want you to."

"All right. We'll call you."

"Thank you."

They watched as he walked away from the booth, and out of the diner, a tall thin man who walked with a slouch, his head slightly bent.

"What the hell," Hawes said, "we *have* to ask the questions."

"Yeah," Carella answered.

"And you've got to admit, Steve, the guy sounds so damn innocent it's implausible."

"What do you mean?"

"Well, for God's sake, his wife is trotting out to see her mother every other week, and spending the night there, and he never even calls to check up? I don't buy it."

"You're not married," Carella said simply.

"Huh?"

"I don't ask Teddy to give me a written report on her whereabouts. You either trust somebody or you don't."

"And he trusted her, huh?"

"It sounds that way to me."

"She was a fine one to trust," Hawes said.

"There are more things in heaven and hell, Horatio," Carella misquoted, "than are dreamt of in your philosophy."

"Like what?" Hawes asked.

22

"Like love," Carella answered.

"Exactly. And you have to admit this thing has all the earmarks of a love pact."

"I don't know."

"Unless, of course, it's a homicide."

"I don't know. I don't know what to accept or reject. All I know is it makes me itchy to have to talk to a guy who's grief-stricken when I'm not really sure . . ."

"*If* he's really grief-stricken," Hawes said. "*If* he didn't happen to turn on that gas jet himself."

"We don't know," Carella said.

"That's exactly why we have to ask the questions."

"Sure. And sometimes give the answers." He paused, his face suddenly very serious. "I gave an answer to a girl on a ledge yesterday, Cotton. There was a puzzled, frightened little girl on a ledge, and she was looking for the big answer, and I gave it to her. I told her to jump."

"Oh, for Christ's sake . . ."

"I told her to jump, Cotton."

"She'd have jumped no matter what you told her. A girl who gets out on a ledge twelve stories above the street . . ."

"Were you around last April, Cotton? Do you remember Meyer's heckler, the guy we called the Deaf Man? Combinations and permutations, remember? The law of probability. Remember?"

"What about it?"

"I like to think of what might have happened if I'd said something different to that girl. Suppose, instead of saying, 'Go ahead, jump,' I'd looked at her and said, 'You're the most beautiful girl in the world, and I love you. Please come inside.' Do you think she'd have jumped, Cotton?"

"If she wanted to jump, then no matter . . ."

"Or I wonder what would have happened if you, or Pete, or Bert, or Meyer, or anyone on the squad—anyone but me —had been at that window. Would she have liked your voice better than mine? Maybe Pete could have convinced her to come inside. Maybe . . ."

"Steve, Steve, what the hell are you doing?"

"I don't know. I guess I didn't enjoy questioning Michael Thayer."

"Neither did I."

"It looks very much like a suicide, Cotton."

"I know it does."

"Sure." Carella nodded. "But, of course, we can't be

23

positive, can we? So we have to bully and con and bluff and . . ."

"Come on!" Hawes said sharply, and in the next instant he almost added, "Why the hell don't you go back to the office and hand in your resignation?" But he looked across the table at Carella and saw that his eyes were troubled, and he remembered what had happened only yesterday when Carella had angrily told a young girl to jump. He caught the words before they left his mouth; he did not tell Carella to resign, he did not tell him to jump. Instead, and with great effort, he smiled and said, "Tell you what we'll do. Let's hold up a bank and then go down to South America and live on the beach like millionaires, okay? Then we won't have to worry about *asking* questions, only answering them. Okay?"

"I'll ask Teddy," Carella said, and he smiled thinly.

"Think about it," Hawes said. "Meanwhile, I'll call the squad."

He left the table and went to the phone booth at the far end of the diner. When he returned, he said, "Good news."

"What?" Carella asked.

"They just picked up Fred Hassler."

4

Fred Hassler was enjoying himself immensely. He was a rotund little man wearing a plaid jacket and a bright blue Italian sports shirt. His eyes were bright and blue, too, and they flashed around the squadroom in obvious enjoyment, his feet jiggling in excitement.

"This is the first time in my life I've ever been in a police station," he said. "Jesus, what color! What atmosphere!"

The color and atmosphere at the moment consisted of a man who was bleeding profusely from a knife wound on his left arm which Detective Meyer Meyer was patiently trying to dress while Detective Bert Kling was calling for an ambulance. In addition, the color and atmosphere included a sixty-year-old man who was gripping the meshed wire of the cage —a small locked enclosure in one corner of the squadroom —and shouting, "Let me *kill* the bastard! Let me kill him!" while alternately spitting at anyone who came anywhere near the compact mesh prison. And the color and atmosphere included, too, a fat woman in a flowered house dress who was complaining to Hal Willis about a stickball game outside her ground-floor apartment, and it included several ringing telephones, and several clattering typewriters, and the contained smell of the squadroom, a delicate aroma compounded of seven-tenths essence of human sweat, one-tenth percolating coffee, one-tenth stench of urine from the old man in the cage, and one-tenth cheap perfume from the fat lady in the flowered house dress.

Carella and Hawes walked into all this atmosphere and color by negotiating the iron-runged steps that led from the ground floor of the old building, coming down the corridor past the Interrogation Room, the Men's Room, and the Clerical Office, pushing through the gate in the slatted rail divider, spotting Andy Parker talking to a rotund little man in a straight-backed chair, assuming the man was Fred Hassler, and going directly to him.

"It stinks in here," Carella said immediately. "Can't someone open a window?"

"The windows are open," Meyer said. His hands were

25

covered with blood. He turned to Kling and asked, "Are they on the way?"

"Yeah," Kling answered. "Why didn't a patrolman handle this, Meyer? He should have got a meat wagon right on the beat. What the hell does he think this is? An emergency ward?"

"Don't ask me about patrolmen," Meyer said. "I'll never understand patrolmen as long as I live."

"He brings a guy up here with his arm all cut to ribbons," Kling said to Carella. "Somebody ought to talk to the captain about that. We got enough headaches without blood all over the floor."

"What happened?" Carella asked.

"The old *cockuh* in the cage stabbed him," Meyer said.

"Why?"

"They were playing cards. The old man says he was cheating."

"Let me out of here!" the old man screamed suddenly from the cage. "Let me *kill* the bastard!"

"They got to stop playing ball outside my window," the fat lady said to Willis.

"You're absolutely right," Willis told her. "I'll send a patrolman over right away. He'll get them to go to a playground."

"There ain't no playground!" the fat lady protested.

"He'll send them to the park. Don't worry, lady, we'll take care of it."

"You said you'd take care of it last time. So they're *still* playing stickball right outside my window. And using dirty language!"

"Where the hell's that ambulance?" Meyer asked.

"They said they'd be right over," Kling told him.

"Turn on that fan, will you, Cotton?" Carella said.

"It smells like a Chinese whorehouse, don't it?" Parker said. "The old man peed his pants when Genero made the collar. He's sixty years old, you know that? But he sure done a job on that arm."

"Who's going to question him, that's what I'd like to know," Hawes said. "That cage smells like the zoo."

"Genero brought him in," Parker said, "we'll get Genero to do the questioning." He laughed heartily at his own outrageous suggestion, and then abruptly said, "This is Fred Hassler. Mr. Hassler, Detectives Carella and Hawes. They're working on that suicide."

"How do you do?" Hassler said, rising immediately and

grasping Carella's hand. "This is *mar-v*elous," he said, "just *mar-v*elous!"

"Yeah, it's marvelous," Parker said. "I'm getting out of this madhouse. If the boss asks for me, tell him I'm in the candy store on Culver and Sixth."

"Doing what?" Carella asked.

"Having an egg cream," Parker answered.

"Why don't you stick around until the ambulance gets here," Kling suggested. "We've got our hands full."

"You've got more cops in this room than they got at the Academy," Parker said, and he left. The fat lady followed him down the corridor, muttering under her breath about the "lousy police in this lousy city." A patrolman came up-stairs to take the old man from the cage to the detention cells on the ground floor. The old man swung at him the moment they unlocked the cage door, and the patrolman instantly clubbed him with his billet and dragged him limp and unprotesting from the squadroom. The ambulance arrived not five minutes later. The man with the slashed arm told the ambulance attendants that he could walk down the steps and out to the waiting ambulance, but they insisted on putting him onto a stretcher. Meyer washed his hands at the corner sink and sat down wearily at his desk. Kling poured himself a cup of coffee. Carella took off his holster, put it into the top drawer of his desk, and sat down beside Fred Hassler. Hawes sat on the edge of the desk.

"Is it like this all the time?" Hassler asked, his eyes bright.

"Not all the time," Carella said.

"Boy, what excitement!"

"Mmm," Carella said. "Where have you been, Mr. Hassler?"

"I was out of town. I had no idea you guys were looking for me. When I got back to the apartment this morning—*brother!* What a mess! The landlady told me I'd better call you guys. So I did."

"Have you got any idea what happened in your apartment while you were gone?" Hawes asked.

"Well, it blew up, that much I know."

"Do you know who was in it when it blew up?"

"The guy, yeah. The broad, no."

"Who was the guy?"

"Tommy Barlow."

"That his full name?" Hawes asked, beginning to write.

"Thomas Barlow, yeah."

"Address?"

27

"He lives with his brother someplace in Riverhead. I'm not sure of the address."

"Do you know the street?"

"No, I don't know that, either. I've never been there."

"How do you know Tommy, Mr. Hassler?"

"We work together in the same place."

"Where's that?"

"Lone Star Photo-Finishing."

"In this city?"

"Yeah. 417 North Eighty-eighth." Hassler paused. "You wondering about the 'Lone Star'? A guy from Texas started the outfit."

"I see. How long have you been working there, Mr. Hassler?"

"Six years."

"You know Tommy Barlow all that time?"

"No, sir. Tommy's been with the company no more'n two years."

"Were you good friends?"

"Pretty good."

"Is he married?"

"Nope. I told you. He lives with his brother. He's a crippled guy, his brother. I met him once down the place. He walks with a cane."

"Do you know his name?"

"Yeah, wait a minute. Andy . . . ? no, wait a minute . . . Angelo . . . ? something like that, just a minute. Amos! Amos, that's it. Amos Barlow. Yeah."

"All right, Mr. Hassler, what was Tommy Barlow doing in your apartment?"

Hassler grinned lewdly. "Well, like what do you think he was doing?"

"I meant . . ."

"They found him with a naked broad, what do you think he was doing?"

"I meant how'd he happen to be there, Mr. Hassler?"

"Oh. He asked me for the key. He knew I was going out of town, so he asked me if he could use the place. So I said sure. Why not? Nothing wrong with that."

"Did you know he was going there with a married woman?"

"Nope."

"Did you know he was going there with a *woman?*"

"I figured."

"Did he tell you as much?"

"Nope. But why else would he want the key?"

"Would you say he was a good friend of yours, Mr. Hassler?"

"Yeah, pretty good. We been bowling together a couple of times. And also, he helps me with my movies."

"Your movies?"

"Yeah, I'm a movie nut. You know, where I work, we don't process movie film. That's all done by Kodak and Technicolor and like that. We just develop and print stills, you know. Black and white, color, but no movies. Anyway, I got this urge to make movies, you see? So I'm always shooting pictures and then I edit them and splice them and Tommy used to help me sometimes. I got this Japanese camera, you see . . ."

"Help you with *what*? The picture-taking or the editing?"

"That, and the acting, too. I've got a reel almost three hundred feet long that's practically all Tommy. You should see some of my stuff. I'm pretty good. That's why this place knocked me on my ass when I walked in here. What color! What atmosphere! *Mar*-velous! Just *mar*-velous!" Hassler paused. "You think I could come in here and take some pictures sometime?"

"I doubt it," Carella said.

"Yeah, what a shame," Hassler said. "Can you picture that guy's arm bleeding in color? *Boy!*"

"Can we get back to Tommy for a minute, Mr. Barlow?"

"Oh, sure. Sure. Listen, I'm sorry if I got off the track. But I'm a nut on movies, you know? I got the bug, you know?"

"Sure, we know," Hawes said. "Tell us, Mr. Hassler, did Tommy seem despondent or depressed or . . . ?"

"Tommy? Who, Tommy?" Hassler burst out laughing. "This is the original good-time kid. Always laughing, always happy."

"When he asked you for the key, did he seem sad?"

"I just told you. He was always laughing."

"Yes, but when he asked you for the key . . ."

"He asked me, wait a minute, it musta been three days ago. Because he knew I had to go out of town, you see. The reason I had to go out of town is I've got this old aunt who lives upstate and I'm hoping someday when she drops dead she'll leave me her house. She hasn't been feeling too good, and I got a cousin who's got his eye on that house, too, so I figured I better get up there and hold her hand a little before she leaves it to him, you know? So I went up there yesterday, took the day off. Today's Saturday, right?"

"That's right."

"You guys work on Saturdays?"

"We try to, Mr. Hassler," Carella said. "Can we get back to Tommy for a minute?"

"Oh, sure. Sure. Listen, I'm sorry if I got off the track. But that house is important to me, you know? Not that I want the old lady to drop dead or anything, but I sure would like to get my hands on that house. It's a big old place, you know? With lilacs all around . . ."

"About Tommy," Carella cut in. "As I understand it, when he asked you for the key, he seemed his usual self, is that right? Happy, laughing?"

"That's right."

"When did you see him last?"

"Thursday. At work."

"Did he take Friday off, too?"

"Gee, I don't know. Why do you ask?"

"We were just wondering what time he and the girl met. He didn't mention anything about that, did he?"

"No. You'd have to check with the boss, I guess. See whether or not Tommy was off on Friday. That's what I'd do if I was you."

"Thanks," Carella said.

"She was married, huh? The broad?"

"Yes."

"Tough break. Her being married, I mean. I got a rule, you know? I never fool around with married women. The way I figure it, there's plenty of lonely single girls in this city who're just ready to . . ."

"Thanks a lot, Mr. Hassler. Where can we reach you if we need you?"

"At the apartment, where do you think?"

"You're going to be staying there?" Hawes asked incredulously.

"Sure. The bedroom's in fine shape. You'd never even know anything happened. The living room's not too bad, either. That's where I keep all my film. Man, if I'da had it stored in the kitchen, *brother!*"

"Well, thanks again, Mr. Hassler."

"Sure, anytime," Hassler said. He shook hands with both detectives, waved at Meyer Meyer, who acknowledged the wave with a sour nod of his head, and then walked out of the squadroom and down the corridor.

"What's *he* doing?" Meyer asked. "Running for mayor?"

"We could use a mayor in this city," Kling answered.

"What do you think?" Carella asked Hawes.

"One thing," Hawes said. "If Tommy Barlow was planning to commit suicide, why would he use a friend's apartment? People don't go around causing trouble for their friends, especially when they're ready to take the pipe."

"Right," Carella said. "And since when do potential suicides go around happy and laughing?" He shook his head. "It doesn't sound as if Tommy was planning a funeral."

"No," Hawes said. "It sounds as if he was planning a party."

It would have been very simple to call the damn thing a suicide and have done with it. Neither Carella nor Hawes were particularly anxious to whip a dead horse, and there was certainly enough evidence around to indicate that Tommy Barlow and Irene Thayer had done the Endsville bit. There was, after all, a suicide note; there was, after all, the presence of enough illuminating gas to have caused an explosion. In addition, there were two empty whisky bottles in the room, and the nearly naked condition of the bodies seemed to strongly indicate this was a true love pact, the doomed lovers perhaps indulging themselves in a final climactic embrace before the gas rendered them unconscious and then dead. All these things in combination made it very easy to reach a conclusion. And the conclusion, of course, should have been suicide.

Carella and Hawes, though, were fairly conscientious cops who had learned through years of experience that every case has a feel to it. This "feel" is something intuitive, and impervious to either logic or reasoning. It is something close to insight, something close to total identification with victim and killer alike. When it comes, you listen to it. You can find whisky bottles on the floor, and clothing stacked in neat little piles, and a typewritten suicide note, and an apartment full of illuminating gas; you can add up all these pieces of evidence and come up with an obvious suicide, and the feel tells you it ain't. It's as simple as that.

It was equally simple for the toxicologist attached to the Chief Medical Examiner's office to arrive at his conclusions. Milt Anderson, Ph.D., was not a lazy man, nor was he being particularly negligent. He was, in all fairness, a man who had been practicing legal toxicology for more than thirty years, and who was a professor of forensic toxicology at one of the city's finest universities. He knew his work well, and he performed it with accuracy and dispatch. The detectives wanted to know only three things:

1. The cause of death.
2. Whether or not the couple were intoxicated prior to death.
3. Whether or not the couple had engaged in sexual intercourse prior to death.

No one had asked him to speculate on whether the deaths were accidental, suicidal, or homicidal. He did exactly what he was asked. He examined the victims and reported, as requested, on the three areas of concern to the detectives. But he had also been filled in on the circumstances surrounding the deaths, and these were firmly in his mind as he performed his tests.

Anderson knew there had been an explosion of illuminating gas. He knew that the jets on the gas range in Fred Hassler's apartment had been left opened. He looked at the bright cherry-red color of the body tissues, blood, and viscera and was willing right then and there to call it death by acute carbon monoxide poisoning. But he was being paid to do a job, and he knew that the most accurate and incontestable method for the determination of carbon monoxide in blood was the Van Slyke Manometric Method. Since his laboratory equipment included the Van Slyke apparatus, he went to work immediately on the blood of both victims. In both cases, he found that the carbon monoxide saturation was close to 60 per cent, and he knew that as low a saturation as 31 per cent could have caused fatal poisoning. He drew his conclusion. His conclusion was absolutely correct. Both Irene Thayer and Tommy Barlow had died of acute carbon monoxide poisoning.

Anderson knew that whisky bottles had been found in the apartment bedroom. He concluded, as he knew the detectives would have, that the couple had been drinking before they turned on the gas. But the detectives specifically wanted to know whether or not the couple had been intoxicated, and Anderson was grateful for the fact that the bodies had been delivered to him with reasonable dispatch. Alcohol is a funny poison. It feels very nice going down, and it can make you very gay and happy—but it is oxidized very rapidly in the system and will disappear entirely from the body during the first twenty-four hours after its ingestion. Anderson received both bodies almost immediately after Michael Thayer had identified his wife, less than twenty hours after the deaths had occurred. He realized this was cutting it dangerously close, but if the pair *had* been intoxicated, he was certain he would still find a sizable percentage of alcohol in their brains. Happily, the brain tissue of both bodies was intact and available for testing. If there was one aspect of toxicology (and there were indeed many) that produced the most heated controversy concerning method and results, it was the analysis of ethyl alcohol. The controversy ranged the spectrum from A to Z, and began with that portion or portions of the body which provided the most reliable biologic specimen for testing purposes. Anderson was a brain man. He knew there were toxicologists who preferred muscle tissue, or liver tissue, or even samplings from the kidney or spleen, but whenever a brain was available to him, he preferred that as a source for his tissue samplings. Two undamaged brains were available to him in the bodies of Irene Thayer and Tommy Barlow, and he used portions of those first to run a routine steam distillation test in an attempt to isolate and separate any volatile poisons in the bodies. There were none. Then, since he had already recovered alcohol during the distillation process, he used that same sampling for his quantitative determination tests. There were charts and charts and more charts relating to the percentage of alcohol recovered in the brain, and how much alcohol it took to make a man tipsy, or staggering, or reeling, or crocked, or downright fall-down, blind, stoned, inert, dead drunk. He had found only the faintest trace of alcohol in each of the brains, and he knew that *whichever* chart he used, neither of the victims would have come anywhere near to being drunk or even mildly intoxicated. But Anderson preferred using a chart based on the findings of Gettler and Tiber who had examined the organs of six thousand alcoholic corpses in an attempt to record degrees of drunkenness. Dutifully, he looked at that chart now:

CLASSI-FICATION	PERCENTAGE OF ALCOHOL IN THE BRAIN		PHYSIOLOGIC EFFECTS
1. Trace	0.005	to 0.02	Normal
2. +	0.02	to 0.10	Normal
3. + +	0.10	to 0.25	Less sense of care.
4. + + +	0.25	to 0.40	Less sense of equilibrium.
5. + + + +	0.40	to 0.60	Unbalance, intoxication.

Dutifully, he decided that the answer to the second question posed him was a definite, negative, resounding NO. The couple had *not* been intoxicated prior to death.

As conscientious as he was, he didn't even attempt to analyze the body fluids and organs for any traces of non-volatile poisons. He already had his cause of death—acute carbon monoxide poisoning—and the isolation, recovery and identification of another, *and* unknown, poison in the bodies would have been a vast undertaking. Given even a small quantity of any particular drug, given even the tiniest clue to its existence in a corpse, Anderson, who was a competent toxicologist, would have consulted his texts and then chosen the best method of isolating that drug. But drugs, unfortunately, are not catalogued according to their properties. This means that if there is an unknown drug in a corpse, and if the toxicologist has no clue supplied either by the circumstances of the death or by a previous autopsy report, he must run *every* test he can think of in a catch-as-catch-can game of trying to isolate something toxic. The nonvolatile organic poisons ranged from glucosides like oleander and scilla and digitalis, to essentials oils like nutmeg and cedar and rue, to aliphatic hypnotics like barbiturates and hydantoins, to organic purgatives like oleum ricini and cascara sagrada, and then into the alkaloids like opium and morphine and atropine . . . there were plenty, and Anderson was familiar with all of them, but he had not been asked to run such exhaustive tests, and saw no necessity for doing so. He had been asked to find out three things, and he already had the answers to the first two. He began work on the third immediately.

He couldn't understand why the cops of the 87th wanted to know whether or not the victims had been making love before they died. He rather suspected the squad contained a horny bastard somewhere in its ranks, a latent necrophiliac. In any case, they wanted the information, and it was not too difficult to provide it. The situation might have been different if the bodies had reached him later than they did. Sperm, like alcohol, simply isn't present after twenty-four hours have expired. He didn't expect to find any moving cells in Irene Thayer's vaginal tract because he knew this was impossible so many hours after her death. But he could hopefully find immobile spermatozoa even now. He took a wet smear, studied the specimen under a high-power microscope, and found no traces of spermatozoa. Not content to leave it at that (there were too many conditions which could explain the absence of spermatozoa in the vagina even following intercourse) he turned to the body of Tommy Barlow, irrigated the urethral canal with a saline solution, aspirated the fluid back into a syringe, and then studied it under his microscope for traces of sperm. There were none.

Satisfied with his findings, he concluded his report and asked that it be typed up for transmission to the 87th.

The report was couched in medical language, and it explained exactly why Anderson was answering his questions as he answered them, exactly what evidence he had found to back up his opinions. The men of the 87th waded through the language and decided that what it all meant was:

1. Gaspipe.
2. Sober.
3. Unlaid.

The report made them wonder where all that booze had gone, if neither of the victims had drunk it. The report also made them wonder why Tommy and Irene had taken off their clothes, if not euphemistically to "be together" for the last time. It had been a reasonable assumption, up to then, that the pair had made love, then dressed themselves partially, and then turned on the gas. If they had *not* made love, why had they undressed?

Somehow, the men on the squad almost wished they'd never received Anderson's damn report.

5

There is something about big women that is always a little frightening: a reversal of roles, a destruction of stereotype. Women are supposed to be delicate and fragile; everybody knows that. They're supposed to be soft and cuddly and a little helpless and dependent. They're supposed to seek comfort and solace in the arms of strong, clear-eyed resolute men.

The two men who rang the doorbell of Mary Tomlinson's house on Sands Spit were strong, clear-eyed, and resolute.

Steve Carella was six feet tall with wide shoulders, narrow hips, thick wrists and big hands. He did not present a picture of overwhelming massiveness because his power was deceptively concealed in the body of a natural athlete, a man who moved easily and loosely, in total control of a fine-honed muscularity. His eyes were brown with a peculiar downward slant, combining with his high cheekbones to give his face a curiously Oriental look. He was not a frightening man, but when you opened the door to find him on your front step, you knew for certain he wasn't there to sell insurance.

Cotton Hawes weighed a hundred and ninety pounds. He was six feet two inches tall, and his big-boned body was padded with obvious muscle. His eyes were an electric blue, and he had a straight unbroken nose, and a good mouth with a wide lower lip. He carried a white streak in the hair over his left temple, where he had once been stabbed while investigating a burglary. He did not look like the sort of man anyone would want to challenge—even to a game of checkers.

Both men were big, both men were strong. And besides, they were each carrying loaded guns on their hips. But when Mary Tomlinson opened the door of the development house, they both felt slightly inadequate and seemed to shrink visibly on the doorstep.

Mrs. Tomlinson had flaming red hair and flashing green eyes. The eyes and the hair alone would have been enough

36

to present her as a woman of force, but they were accompanied by height and girth, and a granite-like, no-nonsense face. She stood at least five feet nine inches tall inside her doorway, a woman with a large bosom and thick arms, her legs and feet planted firmly to the floor, like a wrestler waiting for a charge. She wore a flowered Hawaiian muumuu, and she was barefoot, and she looked at the detectives with suspicion as they faced her inadequately and timorously showed their shields.

"Come in," she said. "I was wondering when you'd get to me."

She did not deliver the cliché with any sense of unoriginality. She seemed not to know that "I was wondering when you'd get to me" had been spoken by countless fictitious heavies long before she was born, and would probably continue to be spoken so long as heavies existed. Instead, she delivered the line as if she were chairman of the board of General Motors who, having called a meeting, was irritated when some of her executives arrived a little late. She had been expecting the police to get to her, and her only question now was what the hell had taken them so long.

She stamped flatfooted into the house, leaving the door for Hawes to close behind him. The house was a typical Sands Spit development dwelling, a small entrance hall, a kitchen on the left, a living room on the right, and three bedrooms and a bath running along the rear. Mrs. Tomlinson had furnished the place with the taste of a miniaturist. The furniture was small, the pictures on the walls were small, the lamps were small, everything seemed to have been designed for a tiny woman.

"Sit down," she said, and Hawes and Carella found seats in the living room, two small caned chairs in which they were instantly uncomfortable. Mrs. Tomlinson spread her ample buttocks onto the tiny couch opposite them. She sat like a man, her legs widespread, the folds of the muumuu dropping between her knees, her big-toed feet again planted firmly on the floor. She looked at her visitors unsmiling, waiting. Carella cleared his throat.

"We'd like to ask you a few questions, Mrs. Tomlinson," he said.

"I assume that's why you're here," she answered.

"Yes," Carella said. "To begin with . . ."

"To begin with," Mrs. Tomlinson cut in, "I'm in the middle of preparations for my daughter's funeral, so I hope you'll

37

make this short and sweet. *Some*body's got to take care of the damn thing."

"You're handling all arrangements, are you?" Hawes asked.

"Who's *going* to handle it?" she said, her lip curling. "That idiot she lived with?"

"Your son-in-law, you mean?"

"My *son*-in-law," she repeated, and she managed to give the words an inflection that immediately presented Michael Thayer as a fumbling creature incapable of coping with anything more difficult than tying his own shoelaces. "Some son-in-law. The poet. Roses are red, violets are blue, let it be said, happy birthday to you. My *son*-in-law." She shook her massive head.

"I gather you don't like him very much," Carella said.

"The feelings are mutual. Haven't you talked to him?"

"Yes, we've talked to him."

"Then you know." She paused. "Or do you? If Michael said anything kind about me, he was lying."

"He said you don't get along, Mrs. Tomlinson."

"That's the understatement of the year. We hate each other's guts. The bully."

"Bully?" Hawes said. He looked at Mrs. Tomlinson in astonishment because the word seemed thoroughly inappropriate coming from her lips.

"Always shoving his weight around. I hate men who take advantage of us."

"Take advantage?" Hawes repeated, the astonishment still on his face.

"Yes. Women are to be treated with respect," she said, "and cared for gently. And with tenderness." She shook her head. "He doesn't know. He's a bully." She paused, and then reflectively added, "Women are delicate."

Hawes and Carella looked at her silently for several moments.

"He . . . uh . . . he bullied your daughter, Mrs. Tomlinson?"

"Yes."

"How?"

"Bossing her. He's a boss. I hate men who are bosses." She looked at Hawes. "Are you married?"

"No, ma'am."

She turned instantly to Carella. "Are you?"

"Yes, I am."

"Are you a boss?"

"I . . . I don't think so."

"Good. You seem like a nice boy." She paused. "Not

38

Michael. Always bossing. Did you pay the electric bill? Did you do the marketing? Did you do this and that? It's no wonder."

Again, the room was silent.

"It's no wonder *what?*" Carella asked.

"It's no wonder Margaret was going to leave him."

"Margaret?"

"My daughter."

"Oh. Oh, yes," Carella said. "You call her Margaret, do you?"

"That's the name she was born with."

"Yes, but most people called her Irene, isn't that true?"

"Margaret was the name we gave her, and Margaret was what we called her. Why? What's the matter with that name?"

"Nothing, nothing," Carella said hastily. "It's a very nice name."

"If it's good enough for the princess of England, it's good enough for anybody," Mrs. Tomlinson said.

"Certainly," Carella said.

"Certainly," Mrs. Tomlinson agreed, and she nodded her head vigorously.

"She was going to leave him?" Hawes asked.

"Yes."

"You mean divorce him?"

"Yes."

"How do you know?"

"She told me. How do you think I know? Mothers and daughters shouldn't keep secrets from each other I told Margaret anything she wanted to know, and she did the same with me."

"When did she plan on leaving him, Mrs. Tomlinson?"

"Next month."

"When next month?"

"On the sixteenth."

"Why that particular day?"

Mrs. Tomlinson shrugged. "Is something wrong with that day?"

"No, nothing at all. But was there a special reason for picking the sixteenth?"

"I never stuck my nose in my daughter's business," Mrs. Tomlinson said abruptly. Carella and Hawes exchanged a quick glance.

"But yet you're certain about the date," Hawes said.

"Yes. She told me she would leave him on the sixteenth."

"But you don't know why the sixteenth?"

"No," Mrs. Tomlinson said. She smiled suddenly. "Are *you* going to bully me, too?" she asked.

Carella returned the smile. Graciously, he answered, "No, certainly not, Mrs. Tomlinson. We're only trying to get the facts."

"I can give you all the facts," Mrs. Tomlinson said. "The first fact is that my daughter didn't commit suicide. That you can count on."

"How do you know?"

"Because I know my daughter. She was like me. She loved life. Nobody who loves life is going to take her own life, that's for sure."

"Well," Carella said, "all the indications . . ."

"Indications! Who cares about indications? My daughter was vital, energetic. People like that don't commit suicide. Look, it runs in the family."

"Energy?" Hawes asked.

"Energy, right I've got to keep moving all day long. Even sitting here, I'm beginning to feel fidgety, would you believe it? There are nervous types of women, you know. I'm one of them."

"And your daughter was another?"

"Absolutely. Always on the go! Vital! Energetic! Alive! Listen, do you want to know something? Shall I tell you how I am in bed?"

Carella looked at Hawes uncomfortably.

"When I get in bed at night, I can't sleep. All that energy. My hands twitch, my legs, I just can't sleep. I take pills every night. Only way I can relax. I'm like a motor."

"And your daughter was that way, too?"

"Positively! So why take her own life? Impossible. Besides, she was going to leave that bully. She was going to start a *new* life." She shook her head. "This whole thing stinks. I don't know who turned on that gas, but it wasn't Margaret, you can count on that."

"Maybe it was Barlow," Hawes suggested.

"Tommy? Ridiculous."

"Why?"

"Because they were going to get married, that's why. So would either of them turn on the gas? Or leave a stupid note like the one in the apartment? 'There is no other way!' Nonsense! They'd already decided on another way."

"Now, let me get this straight, Mrs. Tomlinson," Carella said. "You *knew* your daughter was seeing Tommy Barlow."

"Of course I knew."

"You didn't try to discourage it?"

"Discourage it? Why the hell would I do that?"

"Well . . . well, she *was* married, Mrs. Tomlinson."

"Married! To that bully? *That* was a marriage? Hah!" Mrs. Tomlinson shook her head. "She married Michael when she was eighteen. What does a girl of eighteen know about love?"

"How old was she now, Mrs. Tomlinson?"

"Almost twenty-one. A woman. A woman capable of making up her own mind." She nodded. "And what she decided to do was to leave Michael and marry Tommy. As simple as that. So why should she kill herself?"

"Are you aware, Mrs. Tomlinson, that your daughter told her husband she was coming to visit you on the day she died?"

"Yes."

"Did she do that often?"

"Yes."

"In effect, then, you alibied her, is that right?"

"Alibied? I wouldn't call it that."

"What would you call it?"

"I would call it two sensitive women helping each other against a bully."

"You keep referring to Mr. Thayer as a bully. Did he ever strike your daughter?"

"Strike her? I'd break every bone in his body!"

"Threaten her then?"

"Never. He's a boss, that's all. Believe me, I was glad she planned to leave him."

Carella cleared his throat. He was uncomfortable in the presence of this big woman who thought of herself as a small woman. He was uncomfortable in the presence of this mother who condoned her daughter's adultery.

"I'd like to know something, Mrs. Tomlinson."

"What's that?"

"Michael Thayer said he called you after he saw your daughter's picture in the newspaper . . ."

"That's right."

". . . and asked you whether she was here."

"That's right."

"Mrs. Tomlinson, if you approved of your daughter's relationship with Barlow, if you disliked Michael so much, why did you tell him she wasn't here?"

"Because she wasn't."

"But you knew she was with Barlow."

"So what?"

"Mrs. Tomlinson, did you *want* Michael to know what was going on?"

"Of course not."

"Then why did you tell him the truth?"

"What was I supposed to do? Lie and say Margaret was here? Suppose he asked to speak to her?"

"You could have invented some excuse. You could have said she'd stepped out for a minute."

"Why should I lie to that louse? Anything he got was coming to him!"

"What do you mean?"

"The divorce, I mean. Margaret leaving him."

"Did he know she planned to leave him?"

"No."

"Did she tell anyone else about this divorce, Mrs. Tomlinson?"

"Certainly. She was seeing a lawyer about it."

"Who?"

"I think that's my daughter's business."

"Your daughter is dead," Carella said.

"Yes, I know," Mrs. Tomlinson said.

And then, for no apparent reason, Carella repeated, "She's dead."

The room, for the space of a heartbeat, fell silent. Up until that moment, even though Mrs. Tomlinson had been in the midst of funeral preparations when they'd arrived, even though the conversation had most certainly dealt with the circumstances of their visit, Carella had had the oddest feeling that Mrs. Tomlinson, that Hawes, that he himself were not really talking about someone who was utterly and completely dead. The feeling had been unsettling, a persistent nagging feeling that, despite references in the past tense, despite allusions to suicide, they were all thinking of Margaret Irene Thayer as being *alive,* as a girl who was indeed about to leave her husband next month to begin a new life.

And so, his voice low, Carella repeated, "She's dead," and the room went silent, and suddenly there was perspective.

"She was my only daughter," Mrs. Tomlinson said. She sat on the sofa that was too small for her, a huge woman with flat feet and big hands and lustreless green eyes and fading red hair, and suddenly Carella realized that she *was* truly tiny, that the furniture she'd surrounded herself with was bought for a small and frightened woman lurking somewhere inside that huge body, a woman who really did need gentleness and tenderness.

"We're very sorry," he said. "Please believe that."

"Yes. Yes, I know. But you can't bring her back to me, can you? That's the one thing you can't do."

"No, Mrs. Tomlinson. We can't do that."

"I was looking at all my old pictures of her yesterday," she said. "I wish I had some pictures of Tommy, too. I have a lot of Margaret, but none of the man she was going to marry." She sighed heavily. "I wonder how many pills I'll have to take tonight," she asked. "Before I can sleep. I wonder."

In the silence of the living room, a small porcelain clock, delicately wrought and resting on a small inlaid end table, began chiming the hour. Silently, Carella counted the strokes. One, two, three, four. The echo of the chimes faded. The room was still again. Hawes shifted his position on the uncomfortable caned chair.

"I've made a hundred lists," Mrs. Tomlinson said. "Of things to do. Michael is of no help, you know, no help at all. I'm all alone in this. If Margaret were only alive to . . ." And then she stopped because the absurdity of what she was about to say suddenly struck her. "If Margaret were only alive to help with her funeral preparations" were the words in her mind and on her tongue, and she swallowed them at once because the presence of death was suddenly very large in that small room. She shivered all at once. She stared at Carella and Hawes in the deepening silence of the room. Outside on the street, a woman called to her child. The silence lengthened.

"You . . . you wanted the lawyer's name," Mrs. Tomlinson said.

"Yes."

"Arthur Patterson. I don't know his address."

"In the city?"

"Yes." Mrs. Tomlinson shivered again. "I'm telling you the truth, you know. Margaret *was* leaving him."

"I believe you, Mrs. Tomlinson," Carella said. He rose suddenly and crossed the room. Gently, tenderly, he took her huge hand between both his own and said, "We appreciate your help. If there's anything we can do, please call us."

Mrs. Tomlinson looked up into the face of the tall man who stood before the couch.

In a very small voice, she said, "Thank you."

6

Arthur Patterson was a man in his middle thirties who had recently shaved off his mustache. Neither Carella nor Hawes knew that Patterson had performed the mustachectomy only two days before, but had they been alert detectives they would have noticed that Patterson touched the area over his upper lip rather frequently. The area looked very much like the stretch of skin above *any* man's upper lip, but it didn't feel that way to Patterson. To Patterson, the tiny stretch of skin felt very large and very naked. He kept touching the area to reassure himself that it wasn't getting any larger or any more naked. He didn't feel at all like himself, sitting there and discussing Margaret Irene Thayer with two men from the police department. If he stared down the sides of his nose, he could see his upper lip protruding and swollen and nude. He felt as if he looked very silly, and he was sure the detectives were smiling at his nakedness. He touched the skin above his mouth again, and then hastily withdrew his hand.

"Yes," he said, "Irene Thayer came to me to see about a divorce."

"Had you ever handled any legal matters for her before, Mr. Patterson?" Carella asked.

"I prepared a will. That was all."

"You prepared a will for Irene Thayer?"

"For both of them actually. The usual thing, you know."

"What usual thing, Mr. Patterson?"

"Oh, you know. 'I direct that all my debts and funeral expenses be paid as soon after my death as may be practicable. All the rest, residue and remainder of my estate, whether real or personal, and wherever situate, I give, devise and bequeath to my wife.' That sort of thing."

"Then in the event of Michael Thayer's death, Irene Thayer would have inherited his entire estate?"

"Yes, that's right. And the reverse was, of course, also true."

"How do you mean?"

"In the event that Michael Thayer survived his wife, well,

44

anything *she* owned would go to him. That was one of the will's provisions."

"I see," Carella said. He paused. Arthur Patterson touched his missing mustache. *"Did* she own anything?"

"I don't know. It doesn't seem likely. She seemed concerned about the expense of getting a divorce."

"She told you this?"

"Yes." Patterson shrugged. "I was in a peculiar position here, you understand. It was Thayer who first came to me about drawing the will. And now I was handling a divorce proceeding for his *wife.* It was an odd feeling."

"You mean, you felt as if you were really *Michael* Thayer's lawyer?"

"Well, not exactly. But . . . let's put it this way . . . I felt as if I were attorney for the Thayer *family,* do you know what I mean? And not for Irene Thayer alone."

"But she nonetheless came to you?"

"Yes."

"And said she wanted a divorce."

"Yes. She was going to Reno next month."

"In spite of the expense involved?"

"Well, that was a serious consideration. She initially came to me to find out what the Alabama divorce laws were. She had heard it was a good jurisdiction. But I advised her against an Alabama divorce."

"Why?"

"Well, they've been getting a little rough down there. In many cases, if it appears that a couple came to the jurisdiction only to get a divorce and not to establish bona-fide residency, the state will void the divorce of its own volition. I didn't think she wanted to risk that. I suggested Mexico to her, where we can get a divorce ruling in twenty-four hours, but she didn't like the idea."

"Why not?"

"I'm not sure. A Mexican divorce is as good as any you can get. But the layman has the mistaken impression that Mexican divorces aren't legal or are easy to upset. Anyway, she didn't go for the idea. So, naturally, I suggested Nevada. Are you familiar with the Nevada divorce laws?"

"No," Carella said.

"Well, they require a six-weeks' residency in the state, and the grounds range from . . . well, adultery, impotence, desertion, nonsupport, mental cruelty, physical cruelty, habitual drunkenness . . . I could go on, but that'll give you an idea."

"On what grounds was she suing for divorce?"

"Mental cruelty."

"Not adultery?"

"No." Patterson paused. "She wouldn't have had to go all the way to Reno if she were claiming adultery, would she? I mean . . . after all . . ." He hesitated again. "I don't know how much of this I should discuss with you. You see, I *did* suggest the possibility of she and her husband seeing a marriage counselor, but she wasn't at all interested in that."

"She wanted a divorce."

"Yes, she was adamant about it." Patterson stroked his lip, seemed to be deciding whether or not he should reveal *all* the information he had, and finally sighed and said, "There was another man involved, you see."

"That would seem obvious, wouldn't it, Mr. Patterson?" Hawes said. "They were found dead together."

Patterson stared at Hawes, and then activated a voice he usually reserved for the courtroom. "The fact that they were found dead together needn't indicate they were planning a future life together. Mr. Barlow . . . I believe that was his name . . . ?"

"Yes, Mr. Barlow, that's right."

"Mr. Barlow may not even have been the man she intended marrying."

"Irene's mother seems to think he was."

"Well, perhaps you have information I do not have."

"Irene never told you the man's name?"

"No. She simply said she was in love with someone and wanted a divorce as quickly as possible so that she could marry him."

"She definitely said that?"

"Yes." Patterson dropped his courtroom voice and assumed the tones of a friendly country lawyer dispensing philosophy around a cracker barrel. "It's been my experience, however, that many women . . . and men, too . . . who are contemplating divorce aren't always sure *why* they want the divorce. That is, Irene Thayer may have thought she was in love with this Barlow person and used that as a reason for escaping from a situation that was intolerable to her."

"Did she *say* it was intolerable?" Hawes asked.

"She indicated that living with Michael Thayer was something of a trial, yes."

"Why?"

"She didn't say."

"How did Mr. Thayer feel about the divorce?" Carella asked.

"I did not discuss it with him."

"Why not?"

"Mrs. Thayer preferred it that way. She said she wanted to handle it herself."

"Did she say why?"

"She preferred it that way, that's all. In fact, she was going to serve him by publication, once she got to Nevada and started the proceedings."

"Why would she want to do that?"

"Well, it's not unusual, you know." He shrugged. "She simply wanted to wait until next month. Considering the fact of the other man, I hardly think . . ."

"Next month *when?*" Hawes asked.

"The end of the month sometime." Patterson tried hard to keep his hands clenched in his lap, but lost the battle. His fingers went up to his mouth, he stroked the stretch of barren flesh, seemed annoyed with himself, and immediately put his hands in his pockets.

"But she was definitely going to Reno next month, is that right?" Carella said.

"Yes." Patterson paused and added reflectively, "I saw her several times. I gave her good advice, too. I don't suppose anyone'll pay me for my work now."

"Doesn't the will say something about settling debts and paying funeral expenses?" Carella said.

"Why, yes," Patterson answered. "Yes, it does. I suppose I *could* submit a bill to Mr. Thayer, but . . ." His eyes clouded. "There's a moral issue here, isn't there? Don't you think there's a moral issue?"

"How so, Mr. Patterson?"

"Well, I *am* his lawyer, too. He might not understand why I withheld information of the pending divorce. It's touchy." He paused. "But I *did* put in all that work. Do you think I should submit a bill?"

"That's up to you, Mr. Patterson." Carella thought for a moment and then said, "Would you remember when she planned to leave, exactly?"

"I don't remember," Patterson said. "If I were sure Mr. Thayer wouldn't get upset, I *would* submit a bill. Really, I would. After all, *I* have office expenses, too, and I did give her a lot of my time."

"Please try to remember, Mr. Patterson."

"What?"

"When she was planning to leave for Reno."

"Oh, I'm not sure. The fifteenth, the twentieth, something like that."

"*Was* it the fifteenth?"

"It could have been. Is the fifteenth a Tuesday? I remember she said it would be Tuesday."

Carella took a small celluloid calendar from his wallet. "No," he said, "the fifteenth is a Monday."

"Well, there was something about the weekend interfering, I don't remember exactly what it was. But she said Tuesday, that I remember for certain. Is the twentieth a Tuesday?"

"No, the twentieth is a Saturday. Would she have said Tuesday, the sixteenth?"

"Yes, she might have."

"Would there have been any reason for this? Was she waiting for you to prepare papers or anything?"

"No, that would all be handled by her counsel in Reno."

"Then leaving on the sixteenth was *her* idea?"

"Yes. But you know, local lawyers don't usually prepare the papers in an out-of-state divorce case. So this wasn't . . ."

"What?"

"I did a lot of work even if it didn't involve the preparation of any legal papers."

"What did you mean about a weekend interfering, Mr. Patterson?" Hawes asked.

"Oh, she said something about having to wait until Monday."

"I thought you said Tuesday."

"Yes, she was leaving on Tuesday, but apparently there was something to be done on Monday before she left. I'm sorry I can't be more specific, but it was only a passing reference, and rather vague, as if she were thinking aloud. But she *was* leaving on the sixteenth, I'm fairly certain about that. And naturally, I put all of my time at her disposal."

"Mr. Patterson," Carella said, "you don't have to convince *us*."

"Huh?"

"That you put in a lot of hard work."

Patterson immediately stroked his upper lip, certain that no one in the world would have dared to talk to him that way if he were still wearing his mustache. "I wasn't trying to convince anyone," he said, miffed but trying hard not to show it. "I *did* do the work, and I *will* submit a bill." He nodded vigorously, in agreement with himself. "I hardly think it should upset Mr. Thayer. The facts of his wife's indiscretion were all over the newspapers, anyway."

"Mr. Patterson, what do you think of that suicide note?" Hawes asked.

Patterson shrugged. "The one they ran in the newspapers? Sensationalism."

"Yes, but did it seem consistent with what Mrs. Thayer was planning?"

"That's a leading question," Patterson said. "Of *course* not. Why would she kill herself after going through the trouble of arranging for a divorce? Assuming Barlow was the man she planned to marry . . ."

"You still seem in doubt," Carella said.

"I'm merely exploring the possibilities. If there were yet another man . . ."

"Mr. Patterson," Carella said, "the *existing* possibilities are confusing enough. I don't think we have to go looking for more trouble than we already have."

Patterson smiled thinly and said, "I thought the police were concerned with investigating *every* possibility. Especially in an apparent suicide that stinks of homicide."

"You *do* believe it was a homicide?"

"Don't you?" Patterson said.

Carella smiled and answered, "We're investigating *every* possibility, Mr. Patterson."

There are many many possibilities to investigate when you happen to run the police lab in a large city. Detective-Lieutenant Sam Grossman ran the laboratory at Headquarters downtown on High Street, and he would have been a very busy fellow even if the 87th didn't occasionally drop in with a case or two. Grossman didn't mind being busy. He was fond of repeating an old Gypsy proverb that said something about idle hands being the devil's something-or-other, and he certainly didn't want his hands to become idle and the devil's something-or-other. There were times, however, when he wished he had six or seven hands rather than the customary allotment. It would have been different, perhaps, if Grossman were a slob. Slobs can handle any number of jobs at the same time, dispatching each and every one with equal facility, letting the chips fall where they may, as another old Gypsy proverb states. But Grossman was a conscientious cop and a fastidious scientist, and he was firmly rooted in the belief that the police laboratory had been devised to help the working stiffs who were out there trying to solve crimes. He took

49

a salary from the city, and he believed that the only way to earn that salary was to do his job as efficiently and effectively as he knew how.

Grossman was a rare man to head a laboratory because in addition to being a trained detective, he was also a damned good chemist. Most police laboratories were headed by a detective without any real scientific training but with a staff of qualified experts in chemistry, physics, and biology. Grossman had his staff, but he also had his own scientific background, and the mind of a man who had long ago wrestled with burglaries, muggings, robberies and anything a precinct detective could possibly encounter in his working day. There were times, in fact, when Grossman wished he were back in a cozy squadroom somewhere, exchanging crumby jokes with weary colleagues. There were times, like today, when Grossman wished he had stood in bed.

He never knew what governing law of probabilities caused the laboratory to be swamped with work at times and comparatively idle at other times. He never knew whether a phase of the moon or the latest nuclear test caused a sudden increase in crimes or accidents, whether people declared a holiday for violence at a specific time of the year or month, or whether some Martian mastermind had decided that such and such a day would be a good time to bug Grossman and his hard-pressed technicians. He only knew that there were days, like today, when there was simply too much to do and not enough people to do it.

An amateur burglar had broken into a store on South Fifteenth by forcing the lock on the rear door. Grossman's staff was now involved in comparing the marks found on the lock with specimen marks made with a crude chisel which the investigating detectives had discovered in the room of a suspect.

A woman had been strangled to death in a bedroom on Culver Avenue. Grossman's technicians had found traces of hair on the pillow, and would first have to compare it with the woman's own hair and, in the likelihood that it was not hers, run tests that would tell them whether the hair had been left by an animal or a human, and—if human—which part of the body the hair had come from, whether it had belonged to a man or a woman, whether it had been dyed, bleached, or cut recently, the age of the person who had carelessly left it behind, and whether or not it had been deformed by shooting, burning or scalding.

A holdup man, retreating in panic when he'd heard the

siren of an approaching squad car, had fired three bullets into the wall of a gasoline station and then escaped. Grossman's technicians were now involved in comparing the retrieved bullets with specimen bullets fired from guns in their extensive file, attempting to determine the make of firearm the criminal had used so that the cops of the 71st could dig into their M.O. file for a possible clue.

A ten-year-old girl had accused the janitor of her building of having lured her into his basement room, and then having forced her to yield to his sexual advances. The child's garments were now being examined for stains of semen and blood.

A forty-five-year-old man was found dead on a highway, obviously the victim of a hit and run. The glass splinters embedded in his clothing were now being compared against specimens from the shattered left front headlight of an abandoned stolen car in an effort to identify the automobile as the one which had struck the man down.

Fingerprints, palm prints, fragmentary impressions of sweat pores, footprints, sole prints, sock prints, broken windows, broken locks, animal tracks and tire tracks, dust and rust and feathers and film, rope burns and powder burns, stains of paint or urine or oil—all were there on that day, all waiting to be examined and compared, identified and catalogued.

And, in addition, there was the apparent suicide the boys of the 87th had dropped into his lap.

Grossman sighed heavily and once again consulted the drawing his laboratory artist had made from an on-the-spot sketch of the death chamber:

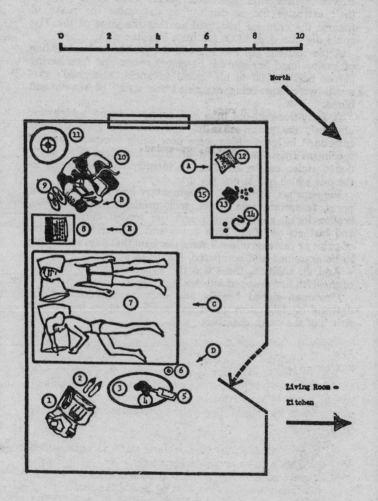

0 2 4 6 8 10

North

Living Room -
Kitchen

In suicide, as in baseball, it is sometimes difficult to tell who is who or what is what without a scorecard. Grossman turned over the lucite-encased sketch and studied the type-written key rubber-cemented to its back:

BEDROOM – APARTMENT 1A

1516 South Fifth Street

1. Chair and woman's clothing.

2. Woman's shoes.

3. Scatter rug.

4. Whisky stain.

5. Whisky bottle, up-ended.

6. Whisky bottle, standing.

7. Bed and victims.

8. End table and typewriter.

9. Man's shoes.

10. Easy chair and man's clothing.

11. End table and lamp.

12. Typewritten note and wrist watch.

13. Wallet, tie clip, loose change.

14. String of pearls, earrings.

15. Dresser.

The little circles containing the letters A, B, C, D, and E, Grossman knew, indicated the camera angles of the photographs taken in the bedroom and enclosed in the folder he now held in his hands. The police photographer had taken, in order:

A. A close shot of the suicide note and the wrist watch holding it down on the dresser top.
B. A medium shot of Tommy Barlow's clothing on the easy chair and his shoes resting beside the chair.
C. A full shot of the bed with the bodies of Irene Thayer and Tommy Barlow lying on it.
D. A medium shot showing the scatter rug and the two

whisky bottles, as well as the chair upon and over which were Irene Thayer's clothes, and beside which were her shoes.

E. A close shot of the typewriter resting on an end table beside the bed.

Grossman studied the sketch and the photographs several times more, reread the report one of his technicians had prepared, and then sat down at a long white counter in the lab, took a telephone receiver from its wall bracket, and dialed Frederick 7-8024. The desk sergeant who answered the telephone connected him immediately with Steve Carella in the squadroom upstairs.

"I've got all this junk on your suicide," Grossman said. "You want to hear about it?"

"I do," Carella said.

"Are you guys busy?"

"Moderately so."

"Boy, this has been a day," Grossman said. He sighed wearily. "What'd they give you as cause of death on this one?" he asked.

"Acute carbon monoxide poisoning."

"Mmm," Grossman said.

"Why? Did you find some spent discharge shells or something?"

"No such luck. It sure *looks* like a suicide, from what we've got here, but at the same time . . . I don't know. There's something not too kosher about this."

"Like what?"

"You'd figure a suicide, wouldn't you?" Grossman said cautiously. "Whisky bottles, open gas jets, an explosion. It all adds up, right? It verifies the figures."

"What figures?"

"On deaths from carbon monoxide poisoning in this city every year. I've got a chart here. Shall I read you what the chart says?"

"Read to me," Carella answered, smiling.

"Eight hundred and forty deaths a year, four hundred and forty of which are suicides. Four hundred and thirty-five of those are from illuminating gas. So it figures, doesn't it? And add the whisky bottles. Suicides of this type will often drink themselves into a stupor after turning on the gas. Or sometimes, they'll take sleeping pills, anything to make the death nice and pleasant, you know?"

"Yeah, nice and pleasant," Carella said.

"Yeah. But there's something a little screwy about this setup, Steve. I'll tell you the truth, I wonder about it."

"What have you got, Sam?"

"Number one, this whole business of the whisky bottles on the floor. Not near the head of the bed, but near the foot. And one of them knocked over. Why were the bottles near the foot of the bed, where they couldn't be reached if this couple had *really* been drinking?"

"They weren't drunk, Sam," Carella said. "Not according to our toxicologist."

"Then where'd all that booze go to?" Grossman said. "And something else, Steve. Where are the glasses?"

"I don't know. Where are they?"

"In the kitchen sink. Washed very nicely. Two glasses sitting in the sink all sparkling clean. Funny?"

"Very funny," Carella said. "If you've turned on the gas and are trying to get drunk, why get out of bed to wash the glasses?"

"Well, they had to get out of bed anyway, didn't they? To put on their clothes."

"What do you mean?"

"Look, Steve, the whole thing smells of a love nest, doesn't it? We checked their garments for seminal stains, and there weren't any. So they must have been naked if they . . ."

"They didn't," Carella said.

"How do you know?"

"Autopsy report. No signs of intercourse."

"Mmmmm," Grossman said. "Then what were they doing with most of their clothes off?"

"Do you want an educated guess?"

"Shoot."

"They probably planned to go out in a blaze of romantic glory. They got partially undressed, turned on the gas, and then were overcome before anything could happen. That's my guess."

"It doesn't sound very educated to me," Grossman said.

"All right, then," Carella said, "they were exhibitionists. They wanted their pictures in the paper without clothes on."

"That not only sounds uneducated, it sounds positively ignorant."

"Give me a better guess."

"A third person in that apartment," Grossman said.

"That's educated, huh?"

"That's highly educated," Grossman said. "Considering the fact that three glasses were used."

"What?"

"*Three* glasses."

"You said two a minute ago."

"I said two in the sink. But we went through the cupboard over the sink, and we checked the glassware there, just because we had nothing else to do, you understand. Most of them were shattered by the blast, but . . ."

"Yeah, yeah, go ahead."

"Light film of dust on all the glasses but one. This one had been recently washed, and then dried with a dish towel we found on a rack under the sink. The lint on the glass compared positive. What do you think?"

"They *could* have used three glasses, Sam."

"Sure. Then why did they leave two in the sink and put the third one back in the cupboard?"

"I don't know."

"A third person," Grossman said. "In fact, when we consider the last, and, I must admit, very very peculiar phenomenon, I'm almost convinced the third person is much more than just an educated guess."

"What's the phenomenon, Sam?"

"No latent impressions in the room."

"What do you mean?"

"No prints."

"Of a third person, do you mean?"

"Of *any*body, I mean."

"I don't understand."

"I'm telling you," Grossman said. "Not a fingerprint on *any*thing. Not on the glasses, not on the bottles, not on the typewriter, not even on their *shoes,* Steve. Now how the hell do you type a suicide note and not leave prints all over the keys? How do you take off a pair of shoes—where there's a good waxy surface that can pick up some beauties—and not leave *some* kind of an impression? How do you pour yourself a drink, and not leave at least a palm print on the bottle? Uh-uh, Steve, it stinks to high heaven."

"What's your guess?"

"My guess is somebody went around that room and wiped off every surface, every article that anybody—especially himself—had touched."

"A man?"

"I didn't say that."

"You said 'himself.' "

"Poetic license. It could have been man, woman, or trained chimpanzee, for all I know. I just finished telling you there's

56

nothing in that apartment, *nothing*. And that's why it stinks. Whoever wiped up the place must have read a lot of stories about how we track down dangerous gunmen because they left behind a telltale print."

"We won't tell them the truth, huh?"

"No, let 'em guess." Grossman paused. "What do you think?"

"Must have been an orgy," Carella said, smiling.

"You serious?"

"Booze, a naked broad—maybe *two* naked broads, for all we know. What else could it have been?"

"It could have been somebody who found them in bed together, clobbered them, and then set up the joint to look like a suicide."

"Not a mark on either one of them, Sam."

"Well, I'm just telling you what I think. I think there was a third party in that room. Who, or why, you'll have to figure out for yourself."

"Thanks."

"Don't mention it. How's the wife and kids?"

"Fine. Sam . . ."

"Mmmm?"

"Sam, not *any* prints? Not a single print?"

"Nothing."

Carella thought for a moment and then said, "They could have wiped the place themselves."

"Why?" Grossman asked.

"Neat. Just as you said. Note neatly typed, clothes neatly stacked, shoes neatly placed. Maybe they were very neat people."

"Sure. So they went around dusting the place before they took the pipe."

"Sure."

"Sure," Grossman said. "Would *you* do that?"

"I'm not neat," Carella said.

7

The combination of Bert Kling and Michael Thayer was a curiously trying one. Hawes liked Kling a hell of a lot, or at least he had liked the Bert Kling he'd known until last year; the new Bert Kling was someone he didn't know at all. Being with him for any length of time was a strange and frustrating experience. This was surely Bert Kling, the same clean young looks, the blond hair, the same voice. You saw him coming into the squadroom or walking down the street, and you wanted to go up to him with your hand extended and say, "Hi, there, Bert, how are you?" You wanted to crack jokes with him, or go over the details of a perplexing case. You wanted to sit with him and have a cup of coffee on days when it was raining outside the squadroom. You wanted to like this guy who was wearing the face and body of Bert Kling, you wanted to tell him he was your friend, you wanted to say, "Hey, Bert, let's get drunk together tonight." You wanted to do all these things and say all these things because the face was familiar, the walk was familiar, the voice was familiar—and then something stopped you dead in your tracks, and you had the feeling that you were only looking at a plastic mold of Bert Kling, only talking to the recorded voice of Bert Kling, that something inside this shell had gone dead, and you knew what the something was, of course, you knew that Claire Townsend had been murdered.

There are different ways of mourning.

When a man's fiancée is the victim of a brutal, senseless massacre in a bookshop, he can react in many ways, all of which are valid, none of which can be predetermined. He can cry his eyes out for a week or a month, and then accept the death, accept the fact that life goes on, with or without the girl he was going to marry one day, life is a progression, a moving forward, and death is a cessation. Bert Kling could have accepted the life surrounding him, could have accepted death as a natural part of life.

Or he could have reacted in another manner. He could have refused flatly to acknowledge the death. He could have gone on living with the fantasy that Claire Townsend was alive and well someplace, that the events which had started with a phone call to the squadroom on the thirteenth of October last year, moved into the shocking discovery of Claire among the victims in the bookshop, and culminated in the vicious beating of the man who'd killed her—he could have gone on pretending, indeed believing that none of these things had happened. Everything was just the way it was. He would continue to wait for Claire's return, and when she came he would laugh with her and hold her in his arms and make love to her again, and one day they would be married. He could have kidded himself in that way.

Or he could have accepted the death without a tear, allowing grief to build inside him like a massive monument, stone added to stone, until the smiling outer visage became the ornate façade of a crumbling tomb, vast, and black, and windswept.

It is perhaps simple for an accountant to evaluate the murder of his fiancée, to go through the tribal custom of mourning, and then to cherish the memory of the girl while philosophically adjusting to the elementary facts of life and death. An accountant adds up columns of figures and decides how much income tax his client owes Uncle Sam. An accountant is concerned with mathematics. Bert Kling was a cop. And being a cop, being involved daily in work which involved crime, he was faced with constant reminders of the girl he had loved and the manner in which she had met her death. It was one thing to walk the streets of the precinct and to cross a six-year-old kid who stood on a street corner waiting for the traffic to pass. It was one thing to be investigating a burglary, or a robbery, or a beating, or a disappearance. It was quite another thing to be investigating a homicide.

The facts of life in the 87th Precinct were too often the facts of death. He had looked into the lifeless eyes of Claire Townsend on October 13th last year, and since that time he had looked into the lifeless eyes of three dozen more victims, male and female, and the eyes were always the same, the eyes always seemed to look up beseechingly as if something had been ripped forcibly from them before they were ready, the eyes seemed to be pleading for that something to be put back, the eyes seemed to beg silently, "Please give it back to me, I wasn't ready." The circumstances of death were always different. He had walked into a room and found a man with a hatchet imbedded in his skull, he had looked down at the eviscerated victim of a hit-and-run, he had opened a closet door and discovered a young girl with a rope knotted about her neck, hanging from the clothes bar, he had found an alcoholic who had drunk himself to death in the doorway of a whorehouse, the circumstances were always different—but the eyes were always the same.

"Please give it back to me," they said. "I wasn't ready."

And each time he looked into a new pair of eyes, he turned away because the image of Claire Townsend on the bookshop floor, her blouse stained a bright red, the book lying open in a tent over her face, his hands lifting the book, his eyes looking into her own dead and staring eyes, this image always and suddenly flared into his mind and left him numb and senseless. He could not think clearly for several moments, he could only turn away from each new corpse and stare at the wall like a man transfixed while a private horror movie ran in the tight projection booth of his mind, reel after reel until he wanted to scream aloud and stopped himself from doing so only by clenching his teeth.

Death meant only one thing to Kling. Death meant Claire Townsend. The daily reminders of death were daily reminders of Claire. And with each reminder, his emotions would close like a fist, tightly clenched; he could not open it, he could not afford to let go. He withdrew instead, retreating from each grisly prod, accepting the burden of memory wearily, refusing sympathy, forsaking hope, foreseeing a future as bleak and as barren as the present.

The equation that day in the tiny office of Michael Thayer in the Brio Building was a simple one. Hawes examined the equation dispassionately, uncomfortable in the presence of Kling and Thayer, recognizing the source of his discomfort, but finding no solace at all in the recognition. Irene Thayer equaled Death equaled Claire Townsend. Such was the elementary equation that seemed to electrify the very air in the small room.

The room was on the sixth floor of the building, its single window open to the April breezes. It contained a desk and a file cabinet and a telephone and a calendar and two chairs. Michael Thayer sat in one of the chairs behind the desk. Hawes sat in the chair in front of the desk. Kling stood tensed like a spring coil alongside Hawes, as if ready to unlock and leap across the desk the moment Thayer said anything contradictory. A stack of completed greeting-card verse rested alongside Thayer's typewriter in a neat, squared pile. A sheet of unfinished doggerel was in the typewriter.

"We work pretty far in advance," Thayer said. "I'm already doing stuff for next Valentine's Day."

"Don't you find it difficult to work so soon after the funeral, Mr. Thayer?" Kling asked.

The question seemed so cruel, so heartlessly devised, that Hawes was instantly torn between a desire to gag Kling and a desire to punch him right in the mouth. Instead, he saw the pain flicker in Thayer's eyes for an instant, and he almost felt the pain himself, and then Thayer said very softly, "Yes, I find it difficult to work."

"Mr. Thayer," Hawes said quickly, "we don't mean to intrude at a time like this, believe me, but there are some things we have to know."

"Yes, you said that the last time I saw you."

"I meant it then, and I mean it now."

"Yes, I'm sure."

"Did you know your wife was going to sue you for divorce?" Kling asked abruptly.

Thayer looked surprised. "No." He paused. "How do you know that?"

"We talked with her lawyer," Hawes said.

"Her lawyer? Art Patterson, do you mean?"

"Yes, sir."

"He never said anything to me about it."

"No, sir, she asked him not to."

"Why?"

"She wanted it that way, Mr. Thayer."

"Mr. Thayer," Kling said, "are you sure you had no inkling that your wife was about to divorce you?"

"None whatever."

"That's a little odd, isn't it? A woman plans to leave you next month, and you haven't got the slightest suspicion that something's in the wind."

"Irene seemed happy with me," Thayer said.

"That's not what her mother said."

"What did her mother say?"

"If I recall the report correctly," Kling said, "Mrs. Tomlinson referred to you as a bully. And a boss." Kling paused. "Did you argue with your wife frequently?"

"Hardly ever."

"Did you ever strike her?"

"What?"

"Strike her, hit her? Did you ever?"

"Never. Of course not."

"Bert . . ."

"Just a second, Cotton, will you? Just a second?" He leveled his impatient gaze on Hawes, and then turned back to Thayer. "Mr. Thayer, you're asking us to believe that there was no friction between you and your wife, while all the time she was playing footsie with . . ."

"I didn't say there was no friction—"

". . . another man and planning to divorce you. Now either you didn't give a damn about her at all, or else . . ."

"I loved her!"

". . . or else you were just plain cockeyed and didn't see what was going on right under your nose. Now which one was it, Mr. Thayer?"

"I loved Irene, I trusted her!"

"And did she love you?" Kling snapped.

"I thought so."

"Then why was she going to divorce you?"

"I don't know. I'm just learning about this. I don't even know if it's true. How do I know it's true?"

"Because we're telling you it's true. She planned to leave for Reno on the sixteenth of May. Does that date mean anything to you, Mr. Thayer?"

"No."

"Did you know she was seeing Tommy Barlow regularly?"

"Bert . . ."

"*Did* you?"

"No." Thayer said.

"Then where did you think she was going every week, every other week?" Kling asked.

"To see her mother."

"Why did her mother call you a bully?"

"I don't know. She doesn't like me. She could have said anything about me."

"How old are you, Mr. Thayer?"

"Thirty-three."

"How old was your wife when she died?"

"Twenty. Well, almost twenty-one."

"How long had you been married?"

"Almost three years."

"She was eighteen when you married her?"

"Yes. Just eighteen."

"And you were how old?"

"Thirty."

"That's a pretty big span, isn't it, Mr. Thayer?"

"Not if two people are in love."

"And you were in love?"

"Yes."

"And you claim you didn't know anything about your wife's boyfriend, or the fact that she was planning to leave you next month?"

"That's right. If I'd known . . ."

"Yes, Mr. Thayer? What would you have done if you'd known?"

"I'd have discussed it with her."

"That's all you'd have done?"

"I'd have tried to talk her out of it."

"And if that failed?"

"I'd have let her go."

"You wouldn't have bullied her or bossed her?"

"I *never* bullied or . . . I was always very good to Irene. I . . . I knew she was much younger than I. I cared for her deeply. I . . . cared for her deeply."

"How do you feel about her now, Mr. Thayer? Now that you know all the facts?"

Thayer hesitated for a long time. "I wish she would have talked it over with me," he said at last. He shook his head. "What she did wasn't the way. She should have talked it over with me."

"Are you a drinking man, Mr. Thayer?" Kling asked suddenly.

"Not . . . well . . . a few drinks every now and then. Not what you'd call a drinking man."

"Did your wife drink?"

"Socially. A Martini now and then."

"Scotch?"

"Sometimes."

"There were two Scotch bottles found in the room with her. Both were empty. One had been knocked over, but the other had apparently been drained. What was the most your wife ever drank?"

"Four drinks. Maybe five. In an evening, I mean. At a party or something."

"How'd she react to liquor?"

"Well . . . she generally got a little tipsy after two or three drinks."

"What would a half-bottle of Scotch do to her?"

"Knock her unconscious, I would imagine."

"Make her sick?"

"Maybe."

"Did liquor ever make her sick?"

63

"Once or twice. She really didn't drink that much, so it's difficult to say."

"The autopsy report showed your wife was not drunk, Mr. Thayer. Yet a full bottle of Scotch, or possibly more, was consumed in that apartment on the day she died. Either consumed or poured down the drain. Which do you think it was?"

"I don't know," Thayer said.

"You just told me your wife didn't drink much. Does killing a bottle of Scotch sound like a thing she would have done?"

"I don't know." He shook his head again. *"Suicide* doesn't sound to me like a thing Irene would have done. *Adultery* doesn't sound to me . . . *divorce* doesn't sound . . . so how do I know what she would or wouldn't have done? I don't know this woman who supposedly killed herself, who had a lover, who was going to Reno. *I don't know her!* So why are you asking me about her? That's not Irene! That's some . . . some . . . some . . ."

"Some what, Mr. Thayer?"

"Some stranger," he said softly. "Not my wife. Some stranger." He shook his head. "Some stranger," he repeated.

The lobby of the Brio Building was crowded with musicians and girl vocalists and dancers and arrangers and song writers and agents who filled the air with the musical jargon of Hip. "Like, man, I told him two bills for the weekend or *adiós,"* a din arising to meet the detectives' ears the moment they stepped from the elevator, "The jerk went and hocked his ax. So I said, like, man, how you expect to blow if you ditched the horn? So he tells me he can't blow anyway unless he's got junk, so he peddled the ax to buy the junk, so now he can't blow anyway, so like what's the percentage?"; bright-eyed girls with bleached-blond hair and loose-hipped dancers' stances, trombone players with long arms and short goatees, agents with piercing brown eyes behind black-rimmed bop glasses, girl singers with hair falling loose over one eye, "Like I said to him, like why should I put out for you if I don't put out for anybody else on the band, and he said like this is different, baby. So I said how is it any different? So he put his hand under my skirt and said this is like love, baby"; a lonely pusher standing on the edges of the crowd, The Man, waiting for an afternoon appointment with a piano player who'd been an addict since the time he was fourteen; a seventeen-year-old girl with a Cleopatra hair-

64

cut waiting to meet a trumpet player who had arranged for an audition with his group; the babble of sound hovering in the air, none of which Kling heard, the pretty girls, overly made up, but pretty with a fresh sparkle in their eyes and with tight light dresses stretched taut over comfortable behinds, none of whom Kling saw; the thronged lobby and the newspaper stand with the tabloids black and bold, the headlines no longer carrying the news of the death of Irene Thayer and Tommy Barlow, both of whom had been shoved off the front page by Khrushchev's latest temper tantrum; they shouldered their way through the crowd, two businessmen who had just completed a business call, and came out into the waning light of a late April afternoon.

"You were too rough with him," Hawes said. He said it suddenly and tersely. He did not turn to look at Kling.

"He may have killed them," Kling answered tonelessly.

"And maybe he didn't. Who the hell are you? The Lord High Executioner?"

"You want to fight with me, Cotton?" Kling asked.

"No. I'm just telling you."

"What are you telling me?"

"I'm telling you there are good cops and shitty cops, and I'd hate to see you become one of the shitty ones."

"Thanks."

"You'd better watch it, Bert."

"Thanks."

They stood on the sidewalk for a moment as the homeward-bound office workers rushed past them. There didn't seem much else to say for the moment. Like polite strangers, they stood with their coats open and their hands in their pockets.

"You going back uptown?" Kling asked.

"I thought *you* might want to type up the report," Hawes said. He paused, and then caustically added, *"You* asked all the questions."

"I guess I did."

"Sure. So you do the report."

"You sore?"

"Yes."

"Screw you," Kling said, and he walked off into the crowd.

Hawes stared after him for a moment, and then shook his head. He took his hands out of his pockets, hesitated, put his hands back into his pockets again, and then walked toward the subway kiosk on the corner.

He was glad to be away from Kling and away from the squadroom. He was glad to be with Christine Maxwell who came in from the kitchen of her apartment carrying a tray with a Martini shaker and two iced Martini glasses. He watched her as she walked toward him. She had let her blond hair grow long since he'd first known her, and it hung loose around the oval of her face now, sleekly reflecting pinpoint ticks of light from the fading sun that filtered through the window. She had taken off her shoes the moment she'd come home from work, but she still wore her stockings and she padded across the room silently, walking with an intuitively feminine grace, insinuatingly female, her straight black skirt tightening over each forward thrust of thigh and leg, the cocktail tray balanced on one long tapered hand, the other hand brushing at an eyelash that had fallen to her cheek. She wore a blue silk blouse that echoed the lilac blue of her eyes, clung loosely to the soft curve of her bosom. She put down the tray and felt his eyes on her and smiled, "Stop it, you make me nervous."

"Stop what?"

"Looking at me that way." Quickly, she poured both glasses full to the brim.

"What way?"

"You're undressing me." Christine handed him one of the Martinis and hastily added, "With your eyes."

"That would be a most impractical way to undress you," Hawes said. "With my eyes."

"Yes, but you're doing it, anyway."

"I'm simply looking at you. I enjoy looking at you." He lifted his glass in the air, said, "Here's looking at you," and swallowed a huge gulp of gin and vermouth.

Christine sat in the chair opposite him, pulling her legs up under her, sipping at her drink. She looked over the edge of the glass and said, "I think you ought to marry me. Then you could look at me all day long."

"I can't marry you," Hawes said.

"Why not?"

"Because good cops die young."

"Then you've got nothing to worry about."

"Are you insinuating I'm not a good cop?"

"I think you're an excellent cop. But you're not exactly young any more."

"That's true. I'm beginning to creak a little in the joints." He paused and said, "But good cops die old, too. In fact, all cops die, sooner or later. Good ones, bad ones, honest ones, crooked ones . . ."

"Crooked cops? The ones who take bribes?"

"That's right. They die, too."

Christine shook her head, a mischievous grin on her mouth. "Crooked cops never die," she said.

"No?"

"No. They're just paid away."

Hawes winced and drained his glass. "I think you went pretty far for that one," he said.

"I think you went pretty far to avoid discussing our imminent marriage."

"Our eminent marriage, you mean."

"I mean imminent, but it'll be eminent, too."

"You know, I have the feeling I'm drunk," Hawes said, "and all I've had is a single drink."

"I'm an intoxicating woman," Christine said.

"Come on over here and intoxicate me a little."

Christine shook her head. "Nope. I want another drink first." She drained her glass and poured two fresh Martinis. "Besides, we were discussing marriage. Are you an honest cop?"

"Absolutely," Hawes said, picking up his drink.

"Don't you think honest cops should seek honest women?"

"Absolutely."

"Then why won't you make me an honest woman?"

"You are an honest woman. Only an honest woman could mix a Martini like this one."

"What's wrong with it, and you're changing the subject again."

"I was thinking of your legs," Hawes said.

"I thought you were thinking of my Martinis."

"That's why it sounded as though I were changing the subject."

"Now *I* feel a little drunk," Christine said. She shook her head, as if to clear it. "How was that again?"

"What's the matter?" Hawes asked. "Don't you dig Ionesco?"

"I not only don't dig him, I also don't understand him."

"Come over here on the couch, and I'll explain Ionesco."

"No," Christine said. "You'll make advances."

"That's right."

"I think a man and a woman should be married before he's permitted to make advances."

"You do, huh?"

"Sure, I do."

"Sure."

"What were you thinking about my legs?" Christine asked.

"How nice they are."

"Nice? That's a fine word to describe a woman's legs."

"Shapely."

"Yes?"

"Well-curved."

"Yes, go on."

"Splendid."

"Splendid?"

"Mmmm. I'd like to take off your stockings," Hawes said.

"Why?"

"So I can touch your splendid legs."

"No advances," Christine said. "Remember?"

"Right, I forgot. I'd like to take off your stockings so I can see your splendid legs better."

"You'd like to take off my stockings," Christine said, "so you can reach up under my skirt to ungarter them."

"I hadn't thought of that, but now that you bring it up . . ."

"*You* brought it up."

"Are you wearing a girdle?"

"Nope."

"A garter belt?"

"Yep."

"I like garter belts."

"All men do."

"Why should all men like garter belts? And how do *you* know what all men like?"

"Are you jealous?"

"No," Hawes said.

"If we were married, I wouldn't have any opportunity to know what all men like," Christine said. "You'd be the only man in my life."

"You mean there are other men in your life?"

Christine shrugged.

"Who are they?" Hawes asked. "I'll arrest them."

"On what grounds?"

"Obstructing the course of true love."

"*Do* you love me?" Christine asked.

"Come here, and I'll tell you."

Christine smiled.

"Come on."

She smiled again. "How long would you say we've known each other, Cotton?" she asked.

"Oh, let me see. Four years?"

"Right. How many times would you say we've made love in those four years?"

"Twice," Hawes said.

"No seriously."

"Oh, seriously. *Seriously*, we've made love . . . how much is four times three hundred and sixty-five?"

"Come on, seriously."

"Gee, I don't know, Christine. Why do you ask?"

"I think we ought to get married."

"Oh," Hawes said, with an air of discovery. "Is *that* what you were leading up to? Ah-ha!"

"Don't you like making love to me?"

"I love making love to you."

"Then why don't you marry me?"

"Come here, and I'll tell you all about it."

Christine stood up abruptly. The move surprised him. A serious look had come onto her face suddenly, and it gave a curious purposefulness to her sudden rise. She walked to the window in her stockinged feet and stood there in silhouette for a moment, the dusky sky outside touching her face with the burnished wash of sunset, and then she pulled down the shade and turned toward Hawes with the same serious expression on her face, as if she were about to cry. He watched her and wondered how this had got so serious all at once. Or perhaps it had been serious all along, he wasn't quite sure now. She took a step toward him and then stopped and looked at him with a long deep look, as if trying to resolve something in her own mind, and then gave a quiet sigh, just a short intake of breath, and unbuttoned her blouse. He watched her in the darkened room as she undressed. She hung the blouse over the back of a straight chair, and then unclasped her brassière and put that on the seat of the chair. She pulled back her skirt and ungartered her stockings, and he watched her legs as she rolled the stockings down over the calves and then the ankles and then rose and put them over the back of the chair and then stood facing him in her panties and garter belt, and then took off the panties and put them on the seat of the chair, too.

She walked toward him in the dim silence of the room, wearing only the black garter belt, and she stopped before him where he sat on the couch, and she said, "I do love you, Cotton. You know I love you, don't you?"

She took his face between both slender hands, and she cocked her head to one side, as if seeing his face for the first time, studying it, and then one hand moved gently to the white streak in his red hair, touching it, and then trailing over his temple, and down the bridge of his nose, and then touching his mouth in exploration in the darkness.

"Nothing to say?" she asked. "Nothing to say, my darling?"

She stood before the couch where he sat, looking down at him with a curiously wistful smile on her mouth. He put his arms around her waist and drew her gently close, cradling his head on her breasts and hearing the sudden frantic beating of her heart, and thinking there really was nothing to say to her, and wondering all at once what love was. He had known her for such a long time, it seemed, had seen her undress in exactly the same way so many times, had held her close to him in just this way, had heard the beating of her heart beneath the full breast. She was Christine Maxwell, beautiful, bright, passionate, exciting, and he enjoyed being with her more than any other person in the world. But holding her close, feeling the beating heart and sensing the wistful smile that still clung to her mouth, and knowing the serious expression was still in her eyes, he wondered whether any of this added up to love, and he suddenly thought of Irene Thayer and Tommy Barlow on the bed in the apartment filled with illuminating gas.

His hands suddenly tightened on Christine's back.

He suddenly wanted to hold her desperately close to him.

She kissed him on the mouth and then sank to the couch beside him and stretched her long legs, and looked at him once more very seriously and then the wistful smile expanded, and she said, "It's because it makes us look French."

"What?" he said, puzzled.

"The garter belt," Christine explained. *"That's* why men like it."

70

8

Tommy Barlow had been a strapping, well-muscled fellow, six feet and one inch tall, weighing a hundred and seventy-five pounds, with a high forehead and a square jaw and an over-all look of understated power. The understated power had been completely muted by death—there is nothing so powerless as a corpse—but even in death, Tommy Barlow bore very little resemblance to his younger brother.

The brother opened the door for Carella and Meyer four days after the burial of Barlow. Both men were wearing trench coats, but not because they wanted to feel like detectives. They wore them only because a light April drizzle was falling.

"Amos Barlow?" Meyer said.

"Yes?"

Meyer flashed the tin. "Detectives Carella and Meyer. We'd like to ask you a few questions."

"Can I see that again, please?" Barlow said.

Meyer, who was the most patient cop in the precinct, if not the entire city, held up his shield again. His patience was an acquired trait, the legacy of his father Max, who'd been something of a practical joker in his day. When Meyer's mother went to Max and told him she was pregnant again, old Max simply couldn't believe it. He thought it was past the time when such miracles of God could happen to his wife, who had already experienced change of life. Unappreciative of the turntable subtleties of a fate that had played a supreme practical joke on the supreme practical joker, he plotted his own gleeful revenge. When the baby was born, he named him Meyer. Meyer was a perfectly good name, and would have fit the child beautifully if his surname happened to be Schwartz or Goldblatt or even Lipschitz. Unfortunately, his surname was Meyer, and in combination with his given name, the infant emerged like a stutter: Meyer Meyer. Even so, the name wouldn't have been so bad if the family hadn't been Orthodox Jews living in a predominatingly Gentile neighborhood. Whenever any of the kids needed an excuse for beating up a Jew—and they didn't often need excuses—it was always easiest to find the one with the double-barreled monicker. Meyer Meyer learned patience: patience toward the father who had inflicted upon him the redundant name, patience toward the kids who regularly sent him home in tatters. Patiently, he waited for the day when *he* could name his *father* Max Max. It never came. Patiently, he waited for the day when he could catch one of the *goyim* alone and beat hell out of him in a fair fight without overwhelming odds. That day came rarely. But Meyer's patience became a way of life, and eventually he adjusted to his father's little gag, and the name he would carry to the end of his days. He adjusted beautifully. Unless one chose to mention the tired old saw about repression leaving its scars. Maybe something *does* have to give, who knows? Meyer Meyer, though he was only thirty-seven years old, was completely bald.

Patiently, he held up the shield.

"Do you have an identification card?"

Meyer dug into his wallet patiently and held up his lucite-encased I.D. card.

"That isn't a very good picture," Barlow said.

"No," Meyer admitted.

"But I guess it's you. What did you want to ask me?"

"May we come in?" Meyer said. They were standing outside on the front stoop of the two-story frame house in Riverhead, and whereas the rain wasn't heavy, it was sharp and penetrating. Barlow studied them for a moment, and then said, "Of course," and opened the door wide. They followed him into the house.

He was a short, slight man, no more than five feet eight inches tall, weighing about a hundred and thirty-five pounds. Carella estimated that he was no older than twenty-two or twenty-three, and yet he was beginning to lose the hair at the back of his head. He walked at a slightly crooked angle and with a decided limp. He carried a cane in his right hand, and he used it as though he'd been familiar with it for a long long time. The cane was black, Carella noticed, a heavy cane with curving head ornately decorated with silver or pewter, it was difficult to tell which.

"Are you the detectives working on my brother's murder?" Barlow said over his shoulder as he led them toward the living room.

"Why do you call it that, Mr. Barlow?" Meyer said.

"Because that's what it was," Barlow answered.

He had entered the living room, walked to the exact

72

center of it, and then turned to face the detectives squarely. The room was tastefully, if inexpensively furnished. He shifted his weight to his good leg, raised his cane, and with it gestured toward a couch. Carella and Meyer sat. Meyer took out a small black pad and a pencil.

"What makes you think it was murder?" he said.

"I know it was."

"How do you know?"

"My brother wouldn't commit suicide," Barlow said. He nodded at the detectives calmly, his pale blue eyes studying them. "Not my brother." He leaned on his cane heavily, and then suddenly seemed tired of standing. Limping, he walked to an easy chair opposite them, sat, looked at them calmly once again, and once again said, "Not my brother."

"Why do you say that?" Carella asked.

"Not Tommy." Barlow shook his head. "He was too happy. He knew how to enjoy life. You can't tell me Tommy turned on the gas. No. I'll believe a lot of other things, but not that."

"Maybe the girl talked him into it," Carella suggested.

"I doubt it," Barlow said. "A cheap pick-up? Why would my brother let her . . . ?"

"Just a second, Mr. Barlow," Meyer said. "This wasn't a casual pick-up, not from the way we understand it."

"No?"

"No. Your brother and this girl were planning to get married."

"Who says so?"

"The girl's mother says so, and the girl's lawyer says so."

"But *Tommy* didn't say so."

"He never mentioned that he was planning to get married?" Carella asked.

"Never. In fact, he never even mentioned this girl, this Irene Thayer. That's how I know it's all a bunch of lies, the note, everything. My brother probably picked the girl up that very afternoon. Marry her! Kill himself! Who are they trying to kid?"

"Who do you mean by 'they,' Mr. Barlow?"

"What?"

"You said. 'Who are *they* trying to . . .'"

"Oh, that's just an expression. I meant, somebody . . . or maybe a couple of people . . ." He shook his head, as if trying to untangle his tongue. "What I mean is Tommy did *not* plan to marry any girl, and Tommy did *not* kill himself. So somebody must have typed up that note and then

73

turned on the gas and left my brother there to die. To *die.* *That's* what I mean."

"I see," Meyer said. "Do you have any idea who this 'somebody' might be?"

"No. But I don't think you'll have to look very far."

"Oh?"

"I'm sure a girl like that had a lot of men after her."

"And you think one of these men might have been responsible for what happened, is that it?"

"That's right."

"Did you know Irene Thayer was married, Mr. Barlow?"

"I read it in the papers."

"But it's your impression that she was seeing other men besides your brother, is that right?"

"She wasn't *seeing* my brother, that's what I'm trying to tell you. He probably just picked her up."

"Mr. Barlow, we have reason to believe he was seeing her regularly."

"What reason?"

"What?"

"What reason? What reason to believe . . ."

"We told you, Mr. Barlow. The girl's mother and the girl's . . ."

"Sure, the girl, the girl. But if Tommy had been seeing her, wouldn't he have told me? His own brother?"

"Were you very close, Mr. Barlow?"

"We certainly were." Barlow paused. "Our parents died when we were both very young. In a car crash. They were coming home from a wedding in Bethtown. That was years ago. Tommy was twelve, and I was ten. We went to live with one of my aunts for a while. Then, when we got old enough, we moved out."

"To this house?"

"No, we only bought this last year. We both worked, you know, from the minute we could get working papers. We've been saving for a long time. We used to live in an apartment about ten blocks from here. But last year, we bought this house. It's nice, don't you think?"

"Very nice," Carella said.

"We still owe a fortune on it. It's more the bank's than it is ours. But it's a nice little house. Just right for the two of us, not too big, not too small."

"Will you keep the house now that your brother's dead?" Meyer asked.

"I don't know. I haven't given it much thought. It's a

74

little difficult to get used to, you know, the idea that he's dead. Ever since he died, I've been going around the house looking for traces of him. Old letters, snapshots, anything that was Tommy. We've been together ever since we were kids, you know. Tommy took care of me as if he was my father. I mean it. I wasn't a strong kid, you know. I had polio when I was a kid."

"I see."

"Yeah, I had polio. It's funny, isn't it, how polio's almost a thing of the past, isn't it? Kids hardly get polio any more, because of the vaccine. But I had it. I was lucky, I guess. I got off easy. I just limp a little, that's all. Did you notice that I limp a little?"

"Just a little," Carella said gently.

"Yeah, it's not too noticeable," Barlow said. He shrugged. "It doesn't stop me from working or anything. I've been working since the time I was sixteen. Tommy, too. From the minute he was old enough to get working papers, Tommy cried when I got polio. I had this fever, you know, I was only seven years old, and Tommy came into the bedroom, bawling his eyes out. He was quite a guy, my brother. It's gonna be funny around here without him."

"Mr. Barlow, are you sure he never mentioned Irene Thayer to you?"

"Yes, I'm certain."

"Is it possible he was withholding the information from you?"

"Why would he do that?"

"I don't know, Mr. Barlow. Perhaps he might have thought you wouldn't approve of his seeing a married woman."

"He *wasn't* seeing her, I've already told you that. Besides, since when did Tommy need *my* approval for anything?" Barlow laughed a short mirthless laugh. "Tommy went his own way, and I went mine. We never even double-dated."

"Then it's possible he *was* seeing this woman, and you just didn't . . ."

"No."

". . . realize it. Maybe the opportunity to discuss it never came up."

"No."

"Mr. Barlow, we have to believe . . ."

"I'm telling you they're lying. They're trying to cover up for what happened in that room. They're saying my brother was involved with that girl, but it isn't the truth. My brother was too smart for something like . . ." Barlow's eyes sud-

75

denly flashed. "That's right, that's another thing! That's right!"

"What?" Carella asked.

"My brother was no dope, you know. Oh, no. He quit high school to go to work, that's true, but he went to night school afterwards, and he got his diploma. So he was no dope."

"What are you driving at, Mr. Barlow?"

"Well, you saw that phony suicide note, didn't you?"

"We saw it."

"Did you see how they spelled 'ourselves'?"

"How did they spell it, Mr. Barlow?"

"O-U-R-S-E-L-F-S." Barlow shook his head. "Not my brother. My brother knew how to spell."

"Maybe the girl typed the note," Meyer suggested.

"My brother wouldn't have let her type it wrong. Look, my brother wouldn't have let her type a note at *all*. My brother just did not commit suicide. That's that. I wish you'd get that into your heads."

"Someone killed him, is that what you think?" Carella asked.

"Damn right, that's what I think!" Barlow paused, and then studied the detectives slyly. "Isn't that what *you* think, too?"

"We're not sure, Mr. Barlow."

"No? Then why are you here? If you really thought this was a suicide, why are you going around asking questions? Why don't you just file the case away?"

"We told you, Mr. Barlow. We're not sure yet."

"So there must be something about it that seems a little funny to you, right? Otherwise, you'd forget the whole thing, right? You must get a lot of suicides."

"Yes, we do, Mr. Barlow."

"Sure. But you know as well as I do that this particular suicide isn't a suicide at all. That's why you're still investigating."

"We investigate *all* suicides," Meyer said.

"This is a murder," Barlow said flatly. "Who are we kidding? This is a murder, plain and simple. Somebody killed my brother, and you know damn well that's the case." He had picked up his cane and stabbed it at the air for emphasis, poking a hole into the air each time he said the word "murder" and again when he said the word "killed." He put the cane down now and nodded, and waited for either Carella or Meyer to confirm or deny his accusation. Neither of the men spoke.

"Isn't it? Isn't it murder?" Barlow said at last.

"Maybe," Carella said.

"No maybes about it. You didn't know my brother. I knew him all my life, There wasn't a man alive who enjoyed living more than he did. Nobody with that much . . . that much . . . *spirit,* yeah, spirit, is going to kill himself. Uh-uh." He shook his head.

"Well, murder has to be proved," Meyer said.

"Then prove it. Find something to prove it."

"Like what, Mr. Barlow?"

"I don't know. There must be something in that apartment. There must be a clue there someplace."

"Well," Meyer said noncommittally, "we're working on it."

"If I can help in any way . . ."

"We'll leave a card," Carella said. "If you happen to think of anything your brother mentioned, anything that might give us a lead, we'd appreciate it."

"A lead to *what?*" Barlow said quickly. "You *do* think it was murder, don't you?"

"Let's say we're making a routine check, shall we?" Carella said, smiling. "Where can we reach you if we need you, Mr. Barlow?"

"I'm right here every night," Barlow said, "from six o'clock on. During the day, you can reach me at the office."

"Where's that?" Meyer asked.

"Anderson and Loeb. That's downtown, in Isola. 891 Mayfair. In the Dock Street section."

"What sort of a firm is that, Mr. Barlow?"

"Optics," Barlow said.

"And what do you do there?"

"I'm in the mailing room."

"Okay," Carella said, "thanks a lot for your time. We'll keep you posted on any developments."

"I'd appreciate it," Barlow said. He rose and began limping toward the door with them. On the front step, he said, "Find him, will you?" and then closed the door.

They waited until they were in the sedan before they began talking. They were silent as they went down the front walk washed with April rain, silent as they entered the car, silent as Carella started it, turned on the wipers, and pulled the car away from the curb.

Then Meyer said, "What do you think, Steve?"

"What do you think?"

Meyer scratched his bald pate. "Well, nobody thinks it was suicide," he said cautiously. "That's for sure."

"Mmmm."

"Be funny, wouldn't it?"

77

"What would?"

"If this thing that everybody's convinced is murder actually turns out to be suicide. That'd be real funny, wouldn't it?"

"Yeah, hilarious."

"You've got no sense of humor," Meyer said. "That's your trouble. I don't mean to bring up personality defects, Steve, but you are essentially a humorless man."

"That's true."

"I wouldn't have mentioned it if it weren't true," Meyer said, his blue eyes twinkling. "What do you suppose makes you such a serious man?"

"The people I work with, I guess."

"Do you find them depressing?" Meyer asked, seemingly concerned.

"I find them obnoxious," Carella confessed.

"Tell me more," Meyer said gently. "Did you really hate your father when you were a small boy?"

"Couldn't stand him. Still can't," Carella said. "You know why?"

"Why?" Meyer asked.

"Because he's essentially a humorless man," Carella said, and Meyer burst out laughing.

9

In police work, "a routine check" is very often something that can hardly be considered routine. A pair of detectives will kick in the front door of an apartment, be greeted by a screaming, hysterical housewife in her underwear who wants to know what the hell they mean by breaking in like that, and they will answer, "Just a routine check, ma'am." A patrolman will pass the stoop of a tenement building and suddenly line up the teen-agers innocently standing there, force them to lean against the wall of the building with their palms flat while he frisks them, and when they complain about their rights, will answer, "Shut up, you punks. This is a routine check." A narcotics cop will insist on examining a prostitute's thighs for hit marks, even when he knows she couldn't possibly be a junkie, only because he is conducting "a routine check."

Routine checks sometimes provide excuses and alibis for anything a cop might feel like doing in the course of an investigation—or even outside the course of one. But there are bona-fide routine checks, especially where suicide or homicide is concerned, and Carella was involved in just such a check on the day he discovered Mary Tomlinson was a liar.

Carella never read mystery fiction because he found it a bore, and besides he'd been a cop for a long, long time and he knew that the Means, the Motive, and the Opportunity were three catchwords that didn't mean a damn when a corpse was staring up at you—or sometimes down at you, as the case might be. He had investigated cases where the motive wasn't a motive at all. A man can push his wife into the river because he thinks he wants to teach her to swim, and you can question him until you're both blue in the face and he'll insist he loved her since they were both in kindergarten and there is simply no Motive at all for his having murdered her. The Means of murder were always fairly obvious, and he couldn't imagine why anyone outside of a motion-picture cop confronted with exotic and esoteric cases involving rare impossible-to-trace poisons got from pygmy tribes would be overly concerned with what killed a person: usually, you found a guy with a bullet hole in the middle of his forehead, and you figured what killed him was a gun. Sometimes, the cause of death was something quite other than what the surface facts seemed to indicate—a girl is found with a knife in her chest, you assume she's been stabbed until the lab tells you someone drowned her in the bathtub first. But usually, if a man looked as if he'd been shot, he'd *been* shot. If a woman looked as if she'd been strangled, she'd *been* strangled. Means and Motive were both crocks to the working cop. Opportunity was the biggest crock of all because every manjack in the U.S. of A., Russia, Madagascar, Japan and the Tasman Sea, Sicily, Greenland, and the Isle of Wight was presented with the Opportunity for committing murder almost every waking minute of his life. The consideration of Opportunity was only valuable in protecting the innocent. A man who was climbing Fujiyama while a murder was being committed in Naples couldn't very well have had an Opportunity for mayhem. The point was, as Carella saw it, that one million, two hundred seventy-four thousand, nine hundred and ninety-nine *other* Neapolitans *did* have the Opportunity for pulling off a bit of homicide that day, and the guy who did the deed certainly wasn't going to tell you he just happened to be with the dead man when it happened. The Means, the Motive, and the Opportunity. *Baloney,* Carella thought, but he nonetheless was calling every insurance company in the city in an attempt to find out whether or not either Tommy Barlow or Irene Thayer had carried life insurance.

He had spoken to twelve insurance companies that morning, had knocked off for lunch when his voice and his dialing finger showed signs of giving out, and had called six more companies since his return to the squad room at 1 P.M. He was dialing his nineteenth company when Meyer said, "What are you doing there on the phone all day?"

"Insurance companies," Carella answered.

"You're a cop. Forget about insurance. The rates are too high."

"It's not for me. I'm trying to . . ." Carella waved Meyer aside with his hand, and said into the phone, "Hello, this is Detective Carella of the 87th Squad. I'd like some information, please."

"What sort of information, sir?"

"Concerning policy holders."

"I'll connect you. Just a moment."

"Thank you." Carella covered the mouthpiece and said to Meyer, "I'm trying to find out if Barlow or the girl were insured."

Meyer nodded, not particularly impressed, and went back to his typing. Carella waited. In a few moments, a man's voice came onto the line. "Mr. Kapistan, may I help you?"

"Mr. Kapistan, this is Detective Carella of the 87th Detective Squad. We're investigating a suicide and are making a routine check of insurance companies in the city."

"Yes, sir?"

"I wonder if you could tell me whether your firm had ever issued policies for either of the two victims."

"What are their names, sir?"

Carella was instantly taken with Kapistan. There was a no-nonsense attitude in the man's voice. He could visualize him immediately understanding everything that was said, could see Kapistan's pencil poised over his pad waiting for the victim's names to be spoken.

"Irene Thayer and Thomas Barlow," Carella said.

"*Miss* Irene Thayer?" Kapistan asked.

"No, that's Mrs. In fact, it's Mrs. *Michael* Thayer. But you might check under her maiden name as well. She was only married for a short time."

"And the maiden name, sir?"

"Irene Tomlinson."

"Can you hold on a moment, Detective Carella?"

"Certainly," Carella said, his respect for Kapistan soaring. He had met too many people who, confronted with any name that ended in a vowel, automatically stumbled over the pronunciation. There was something psychologically sinister about it, he was sure. The name could be a very simple one, like Bruno, or Di Luca, but the presence of that final vowel always introduced confusion bordering on panic. He had had people call the squadroom and, in desperation, finally say, "Oh, let me talk to the Italian cop." Kapistan had only heard the name once, and over a telephone, but he had repeated it accurately, even giving it a distinctive Florentine twist. Good man, Kapistan. Carella waited.

"Mr. Carella?" Kapistan said.

"Yes?"

"I've checked both those names. I have nothing for Thomas Barlow and nothing for Irene Thayer or Mrs. Michael Thayer."

"What about Irene Tomlinson?"

"Is that the exact name? We do have a policy owned by Mrs. Charles Tomlinson for her daughter Margaret Irene Tomlinson, but . . ."

81

"That's the one. Margaret Irene. Who did you say owned the policy?"

"Mrs. Charles Tomlinson."

"Do you have her first name there?"

"Just a moment." Kapistan checked his records. "Yes, here it is. Mary Tomlinson."

"What sort of a policy is it?"

"A twenty-year endowment," Kapistan said.

"In the name of Margaret Irene Tomlinson?"

"That's right. With Mary Tomlinson as payor and bene-ficiary."

"How much?" Carella asked.

"Ten thousand dollars."

"That's not very high."

"Well, that's the cash surrender value of the policy. In addition, there would be about fifteen hundred dollars in ac-cumulated dividends. Just a moment." There was another pause. When he came back onto the line, Kapistan said, "Actually, it's fifteen hundred and fifty dollars."

"Then, if the policy were held to maturity, the company would give eleven thousand five hundred and fifty dollars to the insured."

"Yes, that's right."

"And if the insured died before the policy matured, that money would be paid to the beneficiary, is that right?"

"That's right. Well, not that much money. Only the face value of the policy. Ten thousand dollars."

"To whom?"

"In this case, to the payor, Mary Tomlinson. You know, of course, that when a child reaches the age of fifteen, owner-ship of the policy can be transferred to the child. But that wasn't the case here. No one applied for transfer. That's usually best, anyway. The way some kids behave today . . ." Kapistan let the sentence trail.

"Mr. Kapistan, as I understand it then, Margaret Irene Tomlinson—Mrs. Michael Thayer—was the insured person in a ten-thousand-dollar endowment policy which would have paid her eleven thousand five hundred and fifty dollars upon its maturity, or which will, now that she's dead, pay her mother ten thousand dollars as beneficiary."

"That is right, sir." Kapistan paused. "Detective Carella, I don't mean to impose . . ."

"Go ahead, Mr. Kapistan,"

"You are aware, of course, that there isn't a state in the

82

Union where an insurance company will pay a cent in the event the insured was *killed* by the beneficiary."

"Yes, I know that."

"I thought I might mention it. Please forgive me."

"That's quite all right. Can you tell me when this policy would have reached maturity, Mr. Kapistan?"

"Just a moment, please."

There was another pause.

"Mr. Carella?"

"Yes, Mr. Kapistan?"

"The child was insured on her first birthday. The policy would have matured on her twenty-first birthday."

"Which is next month some time, right?"

"That's right, sir."

"*When* next month?"

"The policy matures on May thirteenth."

Carella had already opened his wallet and pulled out his celluloid calendar. "That's a Saturday," he said.

"That's right, sir."

"Mmm," Carella said. He paused, and then asked, "How does the insured usually collect on an endowment policy when it matures?"

"Usually, they'll write to the company, enclosing the policy, and enclosing some form of identification—usually a photostated birth certificate."

"How long would it take before the company issued a check?"

"Oh, a week, ten days. It's simply a matter of paperwork, provided the proof of identity is satisfactory."

"Suppose the insured were in a hurry? Could it be done sooner?"

"I imagine so."

"How?"

"Well, I suppose the insured could come directly to our office, with the necessary proof of identity, and with the policy. I suppose that would expedite matters."

"Would the company give her a check that very same day?"

"Presumably, yes. If everything were in order."

"Are you open on Saturdays, Mr. Kapistan?"

"No, sir."

"Then, if a policy matured on a Saturday, the insured would have to wait until at least Monday—that would be the fifteenth in this case—before she could come to the office to ask for her check."

83

"'That's right, sir."

"'That explains the weekend interfering," Carella said, almost to himself.

"Sir?"

"I was just thinking aloud. Thank you very much, Mr. Kapistan. You've been most helpful."

"Any time at all," Kapistan answered, "It was nice talking to you. Goodbye."

"Goodbye," Carella said, and he hung up. He sat at his desk for a moment, nodding, smiling, and then he turned to Meyer. "You want to take a ride to the country?" he asked.

"What country?"

"Sands Spit."

"Why?"

"To talk to Mary Tomlinson."

"Why?"

"I want to tell her she's going to be ten thousand dollars richer. I want to see what her reaction is."

What can your reaction be when two bullies march into your living room and tell you they know all about an insurance policy on your dead daughter's life, and want to know why you didn't tell them about it? What can your reaction be when these same two bosses tell you they suspect your daughter wasn't leaving for Reno until the 16th of May because the earliest she could collect on the policy was the 15th of May?

What do you do?

You cry, that's what you do.

Mary Tomlinson began crying.

Meyer and Carella stood in the middle of the miniature living room and watched her quiver and shake as sob after sob wracked her enormous body.

"All right, Mrs. Tomlinson," Carella said.

"I didn't mean to lie," she sobbed.

"All right, Mrs. Tomlinson, let's cut off the tears, huh? We've got a lot of questions to ask you, and we don't want . . ."

"I didn't mean to lie."

"Yeah, but you did."

"I know."

"Why, Mrs. Tomlinson?"

"Because I knew what you'd think."

"And what would we think?"

"You'd think I did it."

84

"Did what?"

"Killed my own daughter. Do you think I'd do that?"

"I don't know, Mrs. Tomlinson. Suppose you tell us."

"I didn't."

"But she was insured for ten thousand dollars,"

"Yes. Do you think I'd kill my own daughter for ten thousand dollars?"

"Some people would kill their own daughter for ten *cents*, Mrs. Tomlinson."

"No, no," she said, shaking her head, the tears streaming down her cheeks. "I *wanted* her to have the money."

"Then why didn't you just sign the policy over to her?"

"I would have, if she'd asked me. But she didn't make her plans until only recently, and we figured it would be just as simple to wait until the thirteenth of next month, when the policy matured. I wanted her to have the money, don't you think I wanted her to have it? I took out the policy when she was just a year old, my husband had nothing to do with it, God rest his soul. I gave it to her for a first birthday present because I figured she could use the money for her education or whatever she wanted to do with it, when she reached the proper age. So don't you think I wanted her to have it? It cost me four hundred and sixty-two dollars and seventy cents a year. Do you think it was easy to scrape together that kind of money, especially after my husband died, poor man?"

"You seem to have managed it, Mrs. Tomlinson."

"It wasn't always easy. But I did it for her, I did it for Margaret. And now you think I killed her to get the money back? No, no, no, no, no, believe me, no, no, no . . ."

"Take it easy, Mrs. Tomlinson." Carella paused. "You should have told us the truth from the beginning."

"You'd have thought the same thing. You'd have thought I killed my own little Margaret."

"Take it easy, Mrs. Tomlinson. *Is* that why she was holding off on the Reno trip? Until she got the policy money?"

"Yes." Mrs. Tomlinson sniffed and nodded.

"Was there any possibility that she *wouldn't* have got that money?"

"What do you mean?"

"Mrs. Tomlinson, your daughter *may* have committed suicide, we don't know. And if she did, she must have had a reason. The note we found said there was no other way, but apparently she'd figured out another way and was ready to get ten thousand dollars that would help make the other way possible. I want to know if anything could have happened, if anything could have been said, or implied, to make her think she *wasn't* going to get that money."

"No."

"Do you know what I'm driving at?"

"Yes. If she thought the money wasn't coming, she might possibly have felt there was no other way out. No. She knew the money was hers. I'd told her about it since the time she was old enough to understand."

"Mrs. Tomlinson," Carella said suddenly. "I'd like to look inside your medicine cabinet."

"Why?"

"Because our man at the lab casually mentioned that your daughter and Tommy Barlow could have been drugged, and I remember you saying something about taking pills every night, and I want to see just what *kind* of pills you've got in that . . ."

"I didn't do anything. I swear on my dead husband, I swear on my dead daughter, I swear on my own eyes, with God as my witness, I didn't do anything. I swear, I swear."

"That's fine, Mrs. Tomlinson, but we'd like to look through your cabinet, anyway."

The medicine cabinet was in the bathroom at the rear of the house. Meyer put down the seat and cover of the toilet bowl, sat, crossed his legs, opened his pad, and got ready to write as Carella opened the cabinet.

"Boy," Carella said.

"What?"

"Full to the brim."

"I'm ready," Meyer said. "Shoot."

"Contents medicine cabinet of Mrs. Charles (Mary) Tomlinson, 1635 Federico Drive, Sands Spit. Top shelf: one bottle aspirin, one bottle tincture merthiolate, one bottle Librium, one container adhesive bandages, one packet bobby pins, one bottle sodium chloride and dextrose, one tube hydrocortisone acetate, one letter opener. You got that?"

"I've got it," Meyer said, writing. "Shoot."

"Second shelf: one bottle Esidrix, one tube Vaseline, one bottle insect repellent, one match book, one tube suntan lotion, one bottle Seconal, one toothbrush, one man's razor, six razor blades new, two razor blades used, one black address book trylon and perisphere gold-embossed on cover, one bottle Demerol APG . . ."

"I just thought of something," Meyer said.

"Yeah, what?"

"If I were J. D. Salinger, listing all this crap in the medicine cabinet would be considered a literary achievement of the highest order."

"It's a shame you're only Meyer Meyer," Carella answered. "Third shelf: one bottle Nytol, three leads from a mechanical pencil, one bottle Fiorinal . . ."

10

Who said they took sleeping pills?" Detective-Lieutenant Sam Grossman wanted to know.

"You said they *might* have," Carella answered. "You said suicides of this type sometimes took sleeping pills, anything to make the death nice and pleasant. Isn't that what you said?"

"All right, all right, it's what I said," Grossman answered impatiently, "but did I ask you to send me fourteen cockamamie bottles of sleeping pills?"

"No, but . . ."

"Steve, I'm up to my ears in work here, and you send me all these sleeping pills. What am I supposed to do with them?"

"I just wanted to know if . . ."

"What'd the necropsy report say, Steve? Did it say anything about sleeping pills?"

"No, but I thought . . ."

"Then what are we supposed to do with these fourteen bottles of pills, would you mind telling me? What do you want me to say about them? Can they put you to sleep? Yes, they can put you to sleep. Would an overdose of any or all of them kill you? Yes, some of them could be fatal if taken in quantity. Okay? Now, what else?"

"I don't know what else," Carella said sheepishly.

"You mean you're reaching for straws already, and the case is barely a week old?"

"All right, I'm reaching for straws. Listen, Sam, you were the one who planted the homicide bug in my head, don't you forget it."

"Who planted? You mean you thought it was suicide?"

"I don't know what I thought, but why not? Why can't it be suicide?"

"Don't get sore with me, Steve-oh."

"I'm not sore."

"What do you want, magic? Okay! Abba-ca-dabbra, whimmity-wham! I see . . . just a moment, the crystal ball is clearing . . ."

"Go to hell, Sam."

"I've got nothing to compare any of these damn pills

against!" Grossman shouted. "Who the hell's going to bother looking for nonvolatile poisons when they've got an obvious case of carbon monoxide poisoning? You know how many stiffs are waiting for autopsy at the morgue? Ahhh, please."

"Somebody *should* have bothered," Carella shouted.

"That's not my department!" Grossman shouted back. "And you happen to be wrong! *Nobody* should have bothered because it would have taken weeks, for Christ's sake, and what would you have got, anyway? So what if they were drugged?"

"That could indicate homicide!"

"It could indicate balls! It could indicate they went to the drugstore and bought some pills and took them, that's what it could indicate. Don't get me sore, Steve."

"Don't get *me* sore!" Carella shouted. "Somebody goofed at the hospital, and you know it!"

"Nobody goofed, and anyway get off my back! Call the goddamn hospital! You want to fight, call them. Did you call me up to fight?"

"I called you up because I sent you fourteen bottles of sleeping pills, and I thought you could help me with them. Obviously, you can't help me, so I'll just say good-bye and let you go back to sleep."

"Look, Steve . . ."

"Look, Sam . . ."

"Ahhh, the hell with it. The hell with it. There's no talking to a bull. I'll never learn. Miracles. You all want miracles. The hell with it."

Both men fell silent.

At last, Grossman asked, "What do you want me to do with these bottles?"

"You know what you can do with them," Carella said.

There was another pause, and then Grossman began laughing. Carella, on the other end of the wire, couldn't suppress his own grin.

"Take my advice," Grossman said, "forget about calling the hospital. They did their job, Steve."

Carella sighed.

"Steve?"

"Yeah, yeah."

"Forget the pills you sent me, too. They're almost all brand names, anyway. Some of them, you don't even need a prescription. Even if the morgue had done those tests and come up with something, you'd be dealing with a pill anybody in the city could have got hold of. Forget it. Take my advice, forget it."

"All right," Carella said. "I'm sorry I blew my stack."

"This is a tough one, huh?"

"Very." Carella paused. "I'm about to hand in my jock."

"You'll settle for suicide?"

"I'll settle for disorderly conduct."

"Not you," Grossman said simply.

"Not me," Carella answered. "Thick-headed. My mother used to call me a thick-headed wop." He paused. "Come on, Sam, help me with those pills. Give me an answer."

"Steve-oh, I don't *have* any."

"We're even," Carella said. He sighed. "You think it was homicide? You still think so?"

Grossman paused for a long time. Then he said, "Who knows? Throw it in the Open File. Come back to it in a few months, in a year."

"Would *you* throw it in the Open File?" Carella asked,

"Me? I'm thick-headed," Grossman said. "My mother used to call me a thick-headed kike." He paused again. "*Yes,* I still think it's a homicide."

"So do I," Carella said.

By the time he left the squadroom at five forty-five that night, he had called every remaining insurance company on his list in an attempt to find out whether Tommy Barlow had been insured. He had drawn a negative response from each company. As he walked to his car parked across the street from the precinct (the sun visor down, the hand-lettered placard clipped to the visor and announcing that this particular decrepit automobile belonged to a cop; please, officer on the beat, do not tag it), he wondered if Tommy Barlow had been insured by a company outside the city. And then he wondered again whether they simply weren't chasing a suicide right into the ground.

He started the car and began driving home toward River-head, reviewing the facts of the case as he drove, driving very slowly and with the windows open because this was April and sometimes—especially in April—Carella felt like seventeen. Jesus, he thought, to die in April. I wonder what the figures on suicide are for April.

Let's examine this thing, he thought. Let's take it from the top for what it obviously is—a suicide. Let's forget there's any such thing as homicide. For the moment, let's simply consider two people who are about to take their own lives, okay? Let's piece it together that way, because none of the other ways seem to fit.

The first thing they had to do was *decide* they were going to kill themselves, which would seem like an odd thing to decide since they'd already made plans for . . .

No, no, wait a minute, he warned himself. Try to find the good reasons for *suicide*, okay? Try to find the things that spell suicide for Tommy Barlow and Irene Thayer, and not what stinks in this case because the things that stink are already there and suffocating me. Jesus, I wish I could take a deep breath. I wish that poor little girl hadn't jumped, I wish to God I could change it, I wish I could reach out and hold her in my arms and say, Honey, please don't jump, honey, please don't throw it all away.

He stopped for a red light.

He stared at the light for a long time, thinking of the young girl on the ledge twelve stories above the street, hearing again the scream that had faded down to the gutter, hearing again the dull empty sound of her body striking the pavement.

The light changed to green.

The image of the dead girl lingered in his mind. Deserted by a man she loved, no apparent reason for staying alive, she jumped. It has to look black. It has to look so goddamn black that there really *is* no other way; it has to appear that death is more comforting than life, it has to be *that* barren and *that* desperate, it has to say exactly what that note in the apartment did say, *there is no other way.*

All right, then, the decision. For some reason—what's the reason?—for some reason, these two, Tommy and Irene have decided that there is no other way, they must end it, they must . . . what did the note say? . . . now we can end the suffering of ourselfs and others. All right, they had decided to end the suffering. *What* suffering? Nobody *knew* about it, damnit. Michael Thayer is a prime candidate for the cuckold of the year, he lets his wife come and go as she pleases, so who the hell knew about it, who were all these other suffering people? Nobody, that's who. Barlow lived with his brother Amos, and Amos knew nothing at all about Irene, so *he* certainly wasn't suffering. Anyway why should he have been suffering even if he did know about his brother's girl? And Mary Tomlinson approved of the affair, so *she* wasn't suffering, so nobody was suffering, so let's take another chorus from the top.

Nobody's suffering.

But the note says end the suffering of ourselfs . . . spelled wrong, have to get some information about Tommy

91

and Irene, the way they spelled, maybe look at some of their letters . . . end the suffering of ourselfs and others. But Tommy and Irene weren't suffering because they were meeting every other week like rabbits, maybe more often, and nobody else was suffering, either, so the note doesn't make any sense.

Unless a few people are lying.

Unless, for example, Thayer *did* know all about his wife's little adventure with young Tommy there, and was all broken up about it, and maybe refused a divorce, and maybe *was* suffering a little. In which case, the note would be accurate, no other way out, suffering, good, we'll turn on the gas.

Or maybe young Amos Barlow knew his brother was seeing Irene and didn't like the idea, told him to stay away from a married woman, told him it broke his heart to see Tommy involved in anything as hopeless as this. In which case, the note would again be accurate, Amos would be suffering, no other way out, good, back to the kitchen and the stove.

Or maybe old Mary Tomlinson, the gentle old genial condoner of her daughter's affair, so she says, maybe *she* didn't like the idea, maybe she told her daughter divorce was a rotten thing, no matter how much of a bully and a boss Thayer was, maybe she said, Darling daughter, stick it through, work it out, this is senseless and it'll break my heart. In which case, note, suffering, ditto, gas.

And in which case, also, everybody happens to be lying.

Which is unreasonable.

Why lie if there's nothing to cover?

Why insist there's been a homicide if they all know Tommy and Irene had good reason to kill themselves? You don't lie to cover up a suicide.

No, wait a minute, I guess you could. I guess you could figure a suicide is a blot on the family escutcheon, something to live down, maybe something hereditary, maybe something that can rub off on all the relatives and friends. Nobody likes the taint of suicide, so maybe they *are* lying about it. Maybe they figure homicide is a much more socially acceptable way to go, a better status symbol. Yes, my poor daughter and her lover were murdered, don't you know? Yes, my poor wife was killed while having an affair, have you heard? Yes, my beloved brother was done in while making love to his mistress. Very posh. Murder is glamorous. Suicide is a drag.

Well, maybe it was a suicide, Carella thought. Maybe they went up there and took off all their clothes—no, not *all* their clothes, they both left their pants on. Propriety. It wouldn't do to be found dead naked, not *stark* naked. They took off some of their clothes, took them off very neatly, stacked them neatly, hung them neatly, of course. Two very neat people. They certainly wouldn't have wanted to be found in a state of nudity. Certainly not. So they left their underwear on for decency's sake, oh Jesus, I am sick to death of Tommy and Irene, I am sick to death of what I see everytime we turn that knob marked homicide and open that rotten goddamn door and find what's inside. I am sick of it, I am sick of it. Why can't they keep themselves private? Why must they parade themselves before everyone to see, exhibit themselves as poor pitiful confused human beings who haven't yet mastered the art of living together? Why must they show the world and each other that all they know how to do is *die* together! Go into your room, lock your door, make your love, and leave us alone! Don't confuse it with illuminating gas and explosions, don't muddy it with blood, keep your goddamn privacy *private!*

He stopped for another light, and closed his eyes for a moment.

When he opened them, his mind had clicked shut again.

He was Detective 2nd Grade Stephen Louis Carella again, shield number 714-56-32.

Tommy got the apartment.

They went up there with two bottles of whisky.

They typed a suicide note.

They turned on the gas.

They took off most of their clothes.

They tried to get drunk, they tried to make love.

The gas reached them before they could accomplish either.

They died.

"This was no goddamn suicide!" Carella said aloud. His own voice startled him. This was no suicide, he repeated silently.

He nodded in the near-darkness of the closed sedan.

This was no suicide.

I want to find out if Tommy Barlow was insured, he thought, and he made an abrupt left turn and began driving toward the house Tommy Barlow had shared with his brother Amos.

93

The house was dark and deserted when he pulled up to the curb in front of it. He thought this was odd because Barlow had told him he was home from work every night at six, and it was now six-thirty, but the house seemed empty and lifeless. He got out of the car. There was a silence to the street, and memory suddenly overtook him in a painfully sweet rush, the memory of his own boyhood street, deserted just before suppertime, a young boy walking toward the house his father owned, his mother calling again from the upstairs window, "Stevie! Supper!" and the slow smiling nod of his head, April. The buds would be opening. The world would be coming alive. He had once seen a cat run over by an automobile, the guts had been strewn all over the gutter, he had turned away in horror, April and the opening buds, April and a cat lying dead in the gutter, matted fur and blood, and the smell of spring everywhere, green, opening.

Barlow's street was quiet. From another block, Carella could hear the sound of the bells on an ice-cream truck. Too early, he thought. You should hit the street after supper, you're too early. The lawn in front of the Barlow house was turning green. The grass was wet. He wanted to reach down suddenly and touch the wet grass. Up the street, he heard the sound of an automobile turning into the block. He went up the front walk and rang the doorbell. There was no answer. He tried it again. He could hear the chimes sounding somewhere deep inside the silent house. A car door slammed somewhere up the street. He sighed and rang the bell a third time. He waited.

Coming down the front steps, he backed several paces away from the house and looked up at the second-story windows. He wondered if Barlow hadn't possibly gone directly into the shower upon returning home from work, and he began walking toward the side of the house, looking for a lighted bathroom window upstairs. He kept to the concrete ribbons of the driveway leading to the garage at the back of the house. A high hedge began on the right of the driveway, leading to the fence of the house next door. He went all the way to the back of the house, looking up at the windows. None of them were lighted. Shrugging philosophically, he started back for his car.

The hedge was on his left now, blocking his view of the street, an effective shield screening the back yard.

As he passed the hedge, he was struck.

The blow came suddenly, but with expert precision. He knew it wasn't a fist, he knew it was something long and hard, but he didn't have much time to consider exactly what it was because it struck him across his eyes and the bridge of his nose and sent him stumbling back against the hedge, and then someone shoved at him, pushing him beyond and behind the hedge as he tried to cover his face with one hand, tried to reach for his revolver with the other. Another blow came. There was a soft whistling sound on the early night air, the sound a rapier makes, or a stick, or a baseball bat. The blow struck him on his right shoulder, hard, and then the weapon came back again, and again there was the cutting whistle and he felt the sharp biting blow on his left shoulder, and his right hand suddenly went numb. His gun dropped to the ground. The end of the weapon gouged into his stomach like a battering ram, and then the sharp edge was striking his face again, repeatedly, numbingly. He lashed out at the darkness with his left hand, there was blood in his eyes, and a terrible pain in his nose. He felt his fist connect, and he heard someone shout, and then his assailant was running away from him, his shoes clattering on the concrete driveway strips, and then on the sidewalk. Carella leaned against the hedge. He heard a car door slamming somewhere up the street, and then the sound of an engine, and then the shrieking of tires as the car pulled away from the curb.

License plate, he thought.

He went around to the other side of the hedge as the car streaked past. He did not see the plate. Instead, he fell forward flat on his face.

11

They picked up Amos Barlow at ten o'clock that night, when he returned to his house in Riverhead. By that time, Carella had been taken to the hospital where the intern on duty dressed his cuts and insisted, over his protests, that he spend the night there. Barlow seemed surprised by the presence of policemen. Neither of the arresting officers told him why the detectives of the 87th wanted to question him. He went along with the two patrolmen willingly and even agreeably, apparently assuming that something had turned up in connection with his brother.

Cotton Hawes greeted him in the squadroom and then led him to the small interrogation room off the entrance corridor. Detectives Meyer and Kling were sitting there drinking coffee. They offered Barlow a cup, which he refused.

"Would you prefer some tea?" Hawes asked.

"No, thank you," Barlow said. He watched the three men, waiting for one of them to say something important, but they were seemingly involved in a ritual they had no desire to disturb. They chatted about the weather, and they cracked a joke or two, but they were mostly intent on consuming their beverage. Hawes finished his tea before the other two men finished their coffee. He put down his cup, took the tea bag from the saucer and dropped it delicately into the cup, and then said, "Where were you all night, Mr. Barlow?"

"Were you trying to reach me?"

"Yes," Hawes said pleasantly. "You told detectives Meyer and Carella that you're usually home by six, but you seemed to be a little late tonight."

"Yes," Barlow said.

"We called your office, too," Meyer put in. "Anderson and Loeb, isn't that right? 891 Mayfair?"

"That's right."

"A cleaning woman answered the phone," Meyer said. "Told us everyone had left."

"Yes, I left the office at about five-thirty," Barlow said.

"Where'd you go then?" Kling asked.

"I had a date."

"Who with?"

"A young lady named Martha Tamid."

"Address?"

"1211 Yarley Street. That's in Riverhead, not far from the Herbert Alexander Oval."

"What time did you pick her up, Mr. Barlow?"

"At about six. Why?"

"Do you drive, Mr. Barlow?"

"Yes."

"Don't you have trouble driving?" Kling asked. "I notice you use a cane."

"I can drive," Barlow said. He picked up the cane and looked at it as if seeing it for the first time. He smiled. "The leg doesn't hinder me. Not when I drive."

"May I see that cane, please, sir?" Hawes asked.

Barlow handed it to him. "Nice-looking cane," Hawes said.

"Yes."

"Heavy."

"Yes."

"Mr. Barlow, did you go home at any time this evening?" Meyer asked.

"Yes."

"When was that?"

"At ten o'clock. Your patrolmen were there. They can verify the time." Barlow looked suddenly puzzled. "I'm sorry, but why are you . . . ?"

"Did you go home at any time *before* ten o'clock?" Meyer said.

"No."

"At, say, six-thirty?" Kling asked.

"No. I didn't get home until ten. I went to pick up Martha directly from the office."

"What'd you do, Mr. Barlow? Go out to dinner? A movie?"

"Dinner, yes."

"No movie?"

"No. We went back to her apartment after dinner."

"Where'd you eat, Mr. Barlow?"

"At a Japanese restaurant in Isola. Tamayuki, something like that. Martha suggested the place."

"Have you known this Martha Tamid long?"

"Just a short while."

"And after dinner you went back to her apartment, is that right?"

"That's right."

"What time was that?"

97

"About eight or eight-thirty."

"And you left there at what time?"

"About nine-thirty."

"You stayed with her for an hour, is that right, Mr. Barlow?"

"About an hour, yes."

"And then you went straight home?"

"That's right," Barlow said.

"And at no time during the night did you go back to the house. Not to check on anything, not to see if you'd left the gas on . . ."

"Is that supposed to be a joke?" Barlow asked vehemently, turning on Kling.

"What?"

"You *know* how my brother died. If you think talking about gas is funny . . ."

"I'm sorry," Kling said. "I wasn't trying to be funny."

"I didn't go back to the house," Barlow said. "I don't know what this is all about. If you don't believe me, call Martha and ask her. She'll tell you anything you want to know. What happened? Was someone else killed?"

"No, Mr. Barlow."

"Then what?"

"Does Miss Tamid have a telephone?" Meyer asked.

"Yes."

"May we have the number, please?" Hawes said.

Miss Martha Tamid lived five blocks away from the Herbert Alexander Oval in Riverhead, a small grass-covered plot of ground in the exact center of which stood a statue of General Alexander astride a horse, looking into the wind with his steely penetrating gaze, his strong jaw, his rugged good looks. Hawes drove past the statue, and then turned into the One Way block called Yarley Street, watching the numbers as he drove, and finally pulling up before 1211. It was almost midnight, but they had called Miss Tamid from the office, and she said she wasn't asleep yet and would be happy to tell them anything they wanted to know. They had told Barlow he could go, but Hawes had nodded at Kling, and Kling had followed Barlow the moment he left the squadroom. Then Hawes had clipped on his holster and begun his drive toward Riverhead.

Miss Tamid lived in a six-story apartment building at the end of the street. She had given Hawes the apartment number on the phone, and he pressed the lobby buzzer for 6C, and then waited for the answering buzz. It came almost instantly.

He let himself in and walked to the elevator. The lobby was small and quiet. The entire building seemed to be asleep at this hour. He went up to the sixth floor, found apartment 6C in the center of the corridor, and rang the bell. He rang it only once, and with a very short ring. The door opened immediately.

Martha Tamid was a tiny girl who looked like an Egyptian belly dancer. Hawes wished he were a private detective because then Miss Tamid would have been in something slinky, or seductive, or both. As it was, she was wearing a blouse and slacks, which was good enough because neither did very much to hide the provocative structure of her tiny body.

"Miss Tamid?" he asked.

"Yes? Detective Hawes?"

"Yes."

"Please, won't you come in? I was waiting for you."

"I'm sorry to be calling so late, but we wanted to check this out as soon as possible."

"That's quite all right. I was watching television. Greta Garbo. She is very good, don't you think?"

"Yes."

Martha Tamid closed the door behind Hawes and led him into her living room. The television set was going with an old Greta Garbo-John Gilbert movie. Miss Garbo was seductively gnawing at a bunch of grapes.

"She is very pretty," Martha said, and then turned off the set. The room was suddenly very still.

"Now then," Martha said, and she smiled.

The smile was a wide one. It lighted her entire face and touched her dark brown eyes, setting them aglow. Her hair was black, and she wore it very long, trailing halfway down her back. She had a small beauty mark near the corner of her mouth, and a dusky complexion he had always associated with Mediterranean peoples. There was an impish quality to her face, the smile, the ignited brown eyes, the tilt of her head, even the beauty mark. There was something else in her face, too, something about her rich body, an open invitation, a challenge, no, that was ridiculous.

He said, "Excuse me, are you a belly dancer?"

Martha laughed and said, "No, I'm a receptionist. Do I look like a belly dancer?"

Hawes smiled. "Well," he said.

"But you have not even seen my belly," Martha said, still laughing, one eyebrow going up just a trifle, just a very slight arching of the brow, but the challenge unmistakable, almost

as if she had said, "But you have not even seen my belly
. . . *yet*."

Hawes cleared his throat. "Where do you work, Miss
Tamid?"

"At Anderson and Loeb."

"Is that where you met Amos Barlow?"

"Yes."

"How long have you known him?"

"I'm only new with the firm," Martha said.

"I'm trying to place your accent," Hawes said, smiling.

"It's a mélange," Martha said. "I was born in Turkey, and
then went from there to Paris, and then to Vienna with my
parents. I have only been here in America for six months,"

"I see. When did you begin working for Anderson and
Loeb?"

"Last month. I was going to school first. To learn typing
and shorthand. Now I know them, so now I am a receptionist."

"Do you live here with your parents, Miss Tamid?"

"No, I am twenty-three years old. That is old enough to
live alone, *n'est-ce pas*, and to do what one desires."

"Yes," Hawes said.

"You are a very big man," Martha said. "Do I make you feel
uncomfortable?"

"No, why should you?"

"Because I am so small," she said. The radiant challenge
came onto her face again. "Though not all over," she added.

Hawes nodded abstractly. "So then . . . uh . . . you met
Mr. Barlow when you started working at Anderson and Loeb
last month."

"Yes." Martha paused. "Would you like something to
drink?"

"No. No, thank you. We're not allowed to on duty."

"A pity," she said.

"Yes."

She smiled briefly, expectantly.

"Did you see Mr. Barlow tonight?" Hawes asked.

"Yes."

"At what time?"

"He picked me up at about six o'clock. Is Mr. Barlow in
some trouble?"

"No, no, this is just a routine check," Hawes said. "What
time did you leave the office, Miss Tamid?"

"At five."

"But *he* didn't leave until five-thirty, is that right?"

"I don't know what time he left. He was still there when I went away, and he arrived here at about six."

"And where did you go then?"

"To a restaurant downtown."

"Why'd you come all the way up here first? You could have gone directly from the office."

"But I had to change my clothes, no?"

"Of course," Hawes said, and he smiled.

"I change my clothes very often," Martha said. "I wore to the office a suit, and then I changed to a dress for my date, and when Amos left, I put on a blouse and slacks, because I do not go to bed until very late."

"I see." He waited, fully expecting her to say, "Would you mind if I changed into something more comfortable now?" but she didn't say it, and of course he knew she wouldn't because what the hell, he was only a city detective and not a private eye.

"What time did you come back here from the restaurant?"

"Eight-thirty, nine o'clock. Somewhere like that."

"And Mr. Barlow left at what time?"

"About nine-thirty, nine forty-five." Martha paused. "Do you find me unattractive?" she asked.

"What?"

"My looks. Are they bad to you?"

"Bad?"

"Not pretty, I mean."

"No, no. No, no, no, you're very pretty."

"I think Amos Barlow didn't think so."

"Why do you say that?"

"I think he was in a hurry to leave me."

"How do you know?"

"Well, I offered him a drink, and he said no. And then I asked him if he liked to dance, and he said no." She paused. Reflectively, she said, "I sometimes don't understand American men."

"Well, it takes all kinds," Hawes said philosophically.

"Do *you* like to dance?"

"Sure."

"But, of course, it's too late to dance now." Martha grinned. "The people downstairs would complain."

"I guess they would," Hawes said.

Martha sighed, inhaling a deep breath, and then exhaling noisily. "He must have thought me unattractive," she said.

"Maybe you're not his type," Hawes said. "Does he date many other girls in the office?"

"I don't know. He is a very quiet man." She shook her head in a delightfully confused way. "I am very frustrated from him."

"Well, all we wanted to know, actually," Hawes said, "was whether or not he really was with you from six to nine-thirty or so. And I guess he was."

"Well, he was *with* me," Martha said, "but whether he was *really* with me, that is an open question." She shrugged. "American men," she said sadly.

"Thank you very much for your help," Hawes said, rising. "I'd better go now. It's getting very late."

"It is never too late," Martha Tamid said cryptically, and she fixed him with a stare so blatant he almost melted. He hesitated for just a moment, wondering, and then walked toward the door.

"Good night, Miss Tamid," he said. "Thank you very much."

"American men," Martha Tamid said, and closed the door behind him.

B.P.I. CLASSIFICATION	(DO NOT FOLD OR ROLL THIS REPORT)	**POLICE DEPARTMENT**	**DETECTIVE DISTRICT** 8th District
Suicide		**SUPPLEMENTARY COMPLAINT REPORT**	**PRECINCT** 87th
THIS CASE WAS CLASSIFIED AS FOLLOWS:		**COPY**	**COMPLAINT NUMBER** 87-10653-21
Suicide			**DATE OF THIS REPORT** 4/18
NAME OF COMPLAINANT People		**ADDRESS OF COMPLAINANT**	4/5 **DATE OF FIRST REPORT**

<u>SURVEILLANCE OF AMOS BARLOW BY DETECTIVE 3rd/GRADE
BERTRAM KLING:</u>

<u>April 12th:</u>

Followed Barlow from precinct to his home in
Riverhead, arrived there 11:08 P.M. Barlow parked
car, 1959 Ford sedan in garage at rear of house, entered house through kitchen doorway at back. Kitchen
light burned for approximately fifteen minutes. At
11:25, light in second story of house went on. Barlow came to window at front of house, looked out into street, drew shade. At 11:35 P.M., upstairs light
went out. Maintained post until 12:30 A.M., at which
time I presumed Barlow had gone to sleep. Put in
call to 64th Precinct, Riverhead, was relieved on
post by Patrolman David Schwartz.

103

<u>April 13th:</u>

      Relieved Schwartz on post at 6:00 A.M. Took
up position on corner of Wagner and Fourteenth,
shielded by hedges of corner house. No sign of activity ~~in~~ at Barlow house until 7:30 A.M. at which time
Barlow came from rear of house, walked to garage,
pulled car out. Followed him to restaurant nearby on
Pike Avenue, place called Family Luncheonette.
Parked across the street, Barlow partly visible
through plateglass front window. He sat at table
alone, ate leisurely breakfast, left luncheonette at
8:22 A.M. Drove through Riverhead via Addison River
Parkway which he picked up at Cannon Road and the
Avenue (Dover Plains Avenue), joining later with River Harb Highway which he took down to Dock Street section. Got off the highway at Land's End, drove Westerly to Mayfair Avenue, parked the car in open lot on
corner of Mayfair and Pickett, walked to office building at 891 Mayfair. No way to continue surveillance
into office, so I checked building for rear exits,
satisfied there were none, and then stationed myself
in lobby near elevator banks. Broke for coffee at
10:15 ~~a.m.~~ A.M., but was able to keep watch of elevators
from lobby drugstore. Barlow came down again at
12:34 P.M., followed him to a restaurant named Fan-
nie's on Pickett Street where he ate lunch alone, and
then walked for about fifteen minutes through small
park outside Criminal Courts Building on MacCauley,

me following. Then back to office again by 1:25 P.M.
I took up position in lobby. Barlow did not emerge
from elevators again until 5:10 P.M. He bought an
evening newspaper at cigar stand, walked to parking
lot, redeemed car, drove directly to River Harb Highway, then onto Addison ~~Parkway~~ River Parkway, exiting
at Cannon Road, and then driving from there to his
house. Parked car in the garage, went into house,
did not come out again all night. I broke for dinner
at 6:50 P.M., relieved by Patrolman Gordley of 64th,
Riverhead, took up post again at 7:45 P.M., relieved
at midnight ~~by~~ again by Gordley.

April 14th:

Barlow followed identical routine as preced-
ing day. There seems to be nothing ~~also~~ at all sus-
picious about ~~him~~ his behavior. His habits seem fixed and quiet.
Doubt very much if he had anything whatever ~~do~~ to do
with beating of Carella.

April 15th:

Saturday morning. Arrived at house earlier
than usual (5:30 A.M.) because I thought Barlow's
Saturday routine might provide something unusual.
Came supplied with coffee and donuts which I had in
the car, parked again on corner of Wagner and Fourteenth, ~~sheild~~ shielded by hedges. Had a long wait. Barlow
apparently sleeps late on Saturdays. He did not come
out of the house until almost twelve noon, by which

time I was hungry all over again. Hoped he would stop for lunch somewhere, but he did not. Instead, he once more drove to Cannon Road and then headed North. Thought for a moment he had tipped to the tail when I lost him in traffic for several blocks. But picked him up again just as he made turn east under elevated structure on Martin. Followed him for five blocks East. He pulled up in front of a florist (Konstantinos Brothers, 3451 Martin Avenue) came out bearing a small floral wreath. Drove East another ten blocks, pulled into gates of Cedarcrest Cemetery. He parked the car in the parking lot, walked to the office, remained there for several moments, and then walked into the cemetery carrying the wreath. I followed him on the path winding through the gravestones. He stopped at one of the stones, stood there for a long time with his head bent, just looking down at the stone. Then he knelt and put the wreath on the grave, and clasped his hands and prayed that way, on his knees, with his hands clasped, for what must have been a full half-hour. He rose, brushed at his eyes as if he'd been crying, and then went back to his car. He stopped for lunch at a diner on Cannon Road (Elevated Diner, 867 Cannon) and then went back to the house in Riverhead, ~~via the park~~ via Dover Plains Avenue. Called the 64th and asked for lunch relief, getting a patrolman named Gleason this time. When I got back to the house at 2:35 P.M., Gleason was gone and so was Barlow. The garage doors were open.

Barlow returned at 3:17 P.M. Gleason pulled
up a few minutes later, driving an unmarked sedan.
Told me Barlow had only gone to do his weekly marketing, stopping at grocer's, butcher's, hardware store,
etc. I thanked Gleason and took up the post again.

Whatever Barlow does with his weekends, he
apparently doesn't go out. This was Saturday night,
but he didn't leave that house again all day. At
11:00 P.M., all the lights went out. I hung around
until one in the morning, and then called the 64th
for relief.

April 16th:

I slept late then checked with Carella at
home to find out where brother Tommy Barlow is buried. Confirmed Cedarcrest. I relieved Patrolman
Gordley on post at 12:15 P.M. Gordley said Barlow
had not been out of the house all morning. At 1:30
P.M., Barlow came out wearing slacks and sweater,
carrying cane. He walked to garage, came out pushing power lawn mower, which he started. He mowed
front lawn, put mower back in garage, went into house
again. At 3:00 P.M., small red compact Chevy II
pulled up in front of Barlow's house. Young girl in
her twenties, long black hair, got out of car, went
up front walk, rang doorbell. I knew Barlow was inside because he hadn't left since mowing the lawn,
but the girl stood on the doorstep and rang the bell

107

for a long time, and he didn't answer the door. She
finally gave up, walked back to the car, angrily
slammed the door, and drove off. Checked immediately
with Hawes for description of Martha Tamid, positive
identification. Asked for relief from 64th, drove to
Miss Tamid's apartment near the Oval. The red compact
was parked at the curb, but when I spoke to her,
she denied having left the apartment, said she'd been
in all day, said she had certainly not driven to Barlow's
house. She offered me a drink, which I declined.
She also asked me if I thought she looked
like an Egyptian belly dancer, which I thought was a
strange question, but I said yes, now that she mentioned
it, I thought she did look like one. She
seems like very aggressive and very female person.
Can't understand her lying about visit to Barlow.

I took up post again at 6:12 P.M., after dinner.
Patrolman said Barlow had not been out. Occurred
to me that perhaps Barlow had left house by
foot, sneaking out back way, leaving his car in the
garage. I called the house from a drugstore two
blocks away, hung up when Barlow answered, took up
post again. Lights went on at 6:45. Lights went out
at 11:00.

I left at 2:00 in the morning, Schwartz relieving.
Schwartz wanted to know why we were sticking
to this guy. I wish I could tell him.

<u>April 17th</u>:

      Monday morning.

      Barlow up and off at 7:30 A.M. Identical
weekday routine. Breakfast, office, lunch, office,
home, lights out, goodnight. Time is now 1:30 A.M.
I left Barlow house at 1:00 A.M., calling 64th for
relief, and getting Gleason who also wanted to know
why we were tailing Barlow.

      Request permission to end surveillance.

Bertram Kling

             Detective 3rd/Grade Bertram Kling

On the morning of April 18th, which was a bright shining Tuesday with the temperature at sixty-three degrees, and the prevailing winds westerly at two miles per hour, Detective Steve Carella left his house in Riverhead and walked toward the elevated structure some five blocks away. He had been attacked on the twelfth of the month but time, as the ancient Arab saying goes, heals all wounds. He had not taken the beating lightly because nobody in his right mind takes a beating lightly. A beating hurts. It is not nice to have someone knock you about the head and the body with a stick or a cane or a baseball bat. It is not nice to be carted off to the hospital where interns calmly look at your bleeding face, and calmly swab the cuts, and calmly dress them as if they are above all this petty bleeding, as if you are a page out of a textbook, elementary stuff, we had this in first year med, give us something hard, like a duodenal ulcer of the Macedonian canal. It is even worse to have to come home and face your wife with all those bandages and chunks of adhesive plaster clinging to your fine masculine head. Your wife is a deaf-mute and doesn't know how to scream, but the scream is there in her eyes, and you wish with all your might that you could erase that scream, that you hadn't been ambushed by some lousy bastard and beaten to a pulp before you could even get your gun in firing position. You wonder how you are going to explain all this to the children in the morning. You don't want them to start worrying about the fact that you are a cop. You don't want them to begin building anxiety neuroses when they're barely out of diapers.

But time heals all wounds—those Arabs knew how to put it all right—and Carella was aware of another old proverb, an ancient Syrian saying that simply stated, "Time wounds all heels." He didn't know who had pounced upon him in the driveway of Barlow's house, but he had every reason to believe that the minions of the law, those stout defenders of the people, those stalwart protectors of the innocent, those relentless tracers of lost persons, those bulwarks of freedom, those citadels of truth and common decency, yeah, he had no doubt the bulls of the 87th would one day pick up some louse who would confess to every crime committed in the past ten years and who would also casually mention he'd happened to beat up a cop named Carella on the night of April twelfth. So Carella was content to bide his time, confident that the odds were on his side. Crime doesn't pay. Everybody knows that. And time is a river.

Time, on that lovely April morning, happened to be a torrential flood, but Carella didn't know that as yet. He was on his way to work, minding his own business on the way to the elevated station, and he hadn't the faintest idea that time was about to reopen a couple of old healed wounds, or that he was about to receive—once again—a few knocks about the head and body. Who expects a beating on a lovely April morning?

The beating came as he was climbing the steps to the elevated platform. The first blow came from behind, and it struck him at the base of the neck, sending him sprawling forward onto the steps. He felt the impact of the sudden shock, felt himself blacking out as he fell forward, and thought only, *Jesus, broad daylight!* and then grasped fumblingly for the steps as he fell. The man with the stick, or the cane, or the baseball bat, or whatever the hell he was using, decided to kick Carella because it was most convenient to kick a man when he was groveling on his knees, grasping for a hold on the steps. So he kicked him in the face, opening one of the cuts there and releasing a torrent of blood that spilled over Carella's cheek and down his neck, and onto his nice white clean go-to-work shirt. A woman coming down the steps screamed and then ran up the steps again, screaming all the way to the change booth, where the Elevated Transit employee tried to calm her down and find out what had happened, while on the steps the man with the stick or the cane or the baseball bat was striking Carella blow after blow on the head and neck, trying his best, it seemed, to kill him. Carella was aware of the woman's screams, and aware of pounding footsteps, and of a man's voice yelling, "Stop that! You stop that, do you hear?" but he was mostly aware of blinding flashes of yellow erupting everywhere the goddamned stick fell, and especially aware of his own dizziness as he groped for his revolver, missing it, feeling the cartridges in his belt, groping again for the handle of the gun, feeling his fingers closing around the walnut stock as his attacker again struck him across the bridge of the nose, *Hit me hard enough you bastard and you'll kill me, hit me on the bridge of the nose and I'll drop dead right here at your feet,* the gun was free.

He swung the gun backhanded, clinging to the steps with one hand, swinging the gun without looking in a wide-armed blind swipe at whoever was behind him. The gun connected. Miraculously, he felt it colliding with flesh, and he heard someone grunt in pain, and he whirled instantly, his back to the steps, and he brought back both feet in an intuitive spring-coil action, unleashing them, the soles of his feet colliding with the man's midriff, sending the man pitching back and down the steps; and all the while Carella was itching to pull the trigger of his gun, all the while he was dying to kill this rotten son of a bitch who was an expert at beating up cops. He got to his feet. The man had rolled to the bottom of the steps, and now he crawled to his knees and Carella leveled the .38 and said, "Stop or I'll shoot!" and he thought, *Go ahead, run. Run and you're dead.*

But the man didn't run. He sat right where he was at the bottom of the steps while the woman at the top continued screaming and the man from the change booth kept asking over and over again, "Are you all right, are you all right?"

Carella went down the steps.

He grabbed the man by the chin, holding the gun muzzle against his chest, and he lifted the man's head and looked into his face.

He had never seen him before in his life.

12

Carella said "No hospital!" and the ambulance driver turned to the intern riding in the back, and the intern looked at Carella and said, "But, sir, you're bleeding rather profusely," and Carella pinned him with his sternest minion-of-the-law stare and said, "No goddamn hospital!" and the intern had the distinct impression that if he'd insisted on this going-to-the-hospital routine, he himself might be the one who went. So he shrugged in his very calm, textbook, intern way, wishing they'd be called some morning to pick up a nice timid old lady with a traumatic subdural hemorrhage instead of a bleeding wildman with a gun in his fist, but those were the breaks, and anyway he'd had all this in first year med. It was better to go to the hospital as a part of the staff, rather than as a patient. So he went.

The man at the bottom of the steps who sat there somewhat sheepishly clutching the area below his stomach, which Carella had kicked with both big feet, wasn't saying very much. His weapon, a sawed-off broom handle, had gone down the steps with him, and Carella picked it up and then bummed a ride from the precinct patrolmen, who had been called—together with the hospital—by the helpful change booth attendant. The patrolmen dropped Carella and his prisoner at the 87th Precinct. Carella, his gun still in his hand, shoved the man across the sidewalk, and up the front steps, and past the muster desk, and up the iron-runged stairway leading to the Detective Division, and down the corridor, and through the slatted rail divider, and then pushed him into a straight-backed chair which, it seemed, was immediately surrounded by detectives.

"You're bleeding," Meyer said to Carella. "You know that?"

"I know it," Carella said. To the man seated in the chair with his head bent, Carella said, "What's your name, mister?"

The man didn't answer.

Carella took the man's jaw between the fingers of one hand, squeezing hard and lifting the man's head, and looking directly into his eyes.

"Your name, mister," he repeated.

The man didn't answer.

112

"Get up."

The man didn't move.

"Get up!" Carella shouted angrily, and he seized the man by the front of the lightweight jacket he was wearing, and then hurled him halfway across the room to the wall alongside the filing cabinets.

"Take it easy, Steve," Meyer cautioned.

Carella holstered his gun, and went through each of the man's pockets. He found a wallet in one of them, and he turned the man around, shoved him into a chair again, and then sat on the edge of a desk as he went through the wallet. Hawes and Meyer stood on opposite sides of the prisoner, waiting. Meyer glanced at Carella, and then shook his head.

"Miscolo!" he yelled.

"Yo!" Miscolo yelled back from the Clerical Office.

"Bring in some iodine and some Band-Aids, will you?"

"Yo!" Miscolo answered.

Carella looked up from the wallet. "Richard Bandler," he said. He looked at the man. "That your name?"

"You're holding my driver's license in your hand, who the hell's name do you think it is?"

Carella flipped the license onto the desk and walked slowly to Bandler and said very slowly and very distinctly, "Bandler, I don't like you very much. I didn't like you the first time you cold-cocked me, and I don't like you any better after the second time. It's all I can do, Bandler, to keep myself from kicking you clear through next Sunday, so you'd better watch your mouth, Bandler, you dig? You'd just better answer everything I ask you nice and peaceful or you're going to be a cripple before they take you to jail, you understand that, Bandler?"

"It seems plain enough," Bandler said.

"It *better* be plain enough," Carella warned. "Is your name Richard Bandler?"

"That's my name."

"Get that tone out of your voice!" Carella shouted.

"What tone?"

"Take it easy, Steve," Hawes said.

Carella clenched his fists, unclenched them, walked back to the desk and picked up the driver's license again. "Is this your correct address? 413 South Sixty-fifth, Isola?"

"No. I've moved since."

"Where to?"

"I'm staying at the Hotel Culbertson downtown."

"How long have you been staying there?"

113

"About ten days."

"You moved from Sixty-fifth Street ten days ago?"

"No. I moved from Sixty-fifth last month."

"Where to?"

Bandler paused.

"Where to, Bandler?"

"The Coast."

"When did you leave?"

"On March twenty-seventh."

"Why? Are you wanted in this city?"

"No."

"Are you wanted *anywhere?*"

"No."

"We're going to check, you know. If you're wanted . . ."

"I'm not wanted. I'm not a criminal."

"Maybe you *weren't* a criminal," Hawes said, "but you are now, mister. First-degree assault happens to be a big fat felony."

Bandler said nothing. Miscolo came in from the clerical office with the adhesive bandages and the iodine. He took a look at Carella's face, shook his head, clucked his tongue, and then said, "Jesus, what's the matter with you, anyway?" He took another look and said, "Go wash your face in the sink there."

"My face is all right, Alf," Carella said.

"Go wash your face," Miscolo said sternly, and Carella sighed and went to the corner sink.

"Have you got a record, Bandler?" Hawes asked.

"No, I told you. I'm not a criminal."

"All right, why'd you go to California?"

"I've got a job there."

"What kind of a job?"

"In television."

"Doing what?"

"I'm an assistant director."

"What do you direct?" Carella said from the sink. He reached for the white towel hanging on a rack and Miscolo yelled, "You'll get that all full of blood. Use the paper towels."

"Assistant directors don't direct very much," Bandler said. "We maintain quiet on the set, we call actors, we . . ."

"We're not interested in an industry survey," Hawes said. "What show do you work on?"

"Well . . . well, you see, I don't actually have a steady job with any one show."

114

"Then why did you go to California?" Meyer said. "You just told us you had a job there."

"Well, I did."

"What job?"

"They were shooting a ninety-minute special. So a friend of mine who was directing the show called to see if I'd like to work with him. As assistant, you see. So I went to the Coast."

Carella came back to the desk and sat on the edge of it. Miscolo picked up the iodine bottle and began swabbing the cuts. "You're gonna need stitches here," he said.

"I don't think so."

"It's the same cut from last week," Miscolo said. "It's opened all over again."

"Why'd you come back from the Coast?" Carella asked.

"The job ended. I looked around for a while, to see if I could get some kind of steady work, but nothing came up. So I came back here."

"Are you working now?"

"No. I just got back about ten days ago."

"When was that, Bandler?"

"The eighth."

"Ow!" Carella said as Miscolo pressed a piece of adhesive in place. "Why'd you come after me, Bandler?"

"Because . . . I found out what you did."

"Yeah? What did I do? Ouch! For Christ's sake, Alf . . ."

"I'm sorry, I'm sorry," Miscolo said. "I'm not a doctor, you know," he added petulantly. "I'm only a lousy clerk. Next time, go to the hospital instead of messing up the whole damn squadroom."

"What did I do?" Carella asked again.

"You killed my girl," Bandler said.

"What?"

"You killed my girl."

For a moment, no one in the room made a connection. They stared at Bandler in silent puzzlement, and then Bandler said, "Blanche. Blanche Mattfield," and the name still meant nothing to anyone but Carella.

Carella nodded. "She jumped, Bandler," he said. "I had nothing to do with her jumping."

"You *told* her to jump."

"I was trying to get her off that ledge."

"You got her off, all right."

"How do you know what I said to her?"

"The landlady told me. She was in the room behind you, and she heard you tell her to jump." Bandler paused and then said, "Why didn't you just shove her off that ledge? It would have amounted to the same thing."

"Do you have any idea why she was on that ledge to begin with?" Carella asked.

"What difference does it make? She wouldn't have jumped if it hadn't been for you!"

"She wouldn't have been out there if it hadn't been for you!" Carella said.

"Sure," Bandler said.

"Why'd you leave her?"

"*Who* left her?"

"You did, you did. Come on, Bandler, don't get me sore again. She wanted to die because you left her. 'Goodbye, Blanche, it's been fun.' Those were your exact words."

"I loved that girl," Bandler protested. "She knew I was coming right back. She knew it was just a temporary job. I told her . . ."

"You walked out on her, Bandler."

"I tell you I didn't. I *loved* her, don't you understand? She knew I was coming back. I told her so. How do I know why she decided to . . . to kill herself?"

"She killed herself because she knew you were finished with her. Do you feel better now?"

"Wh . . . what do you mean?"

"After beating me up? After shoving all the blame onto me?"

"You killed her!" Bandler shouted, and he came out of the chair angrily, and Carella put both hands on his shoulders and shoved him back down again.

"What's the name of this friend of yours on the Coast?"

"Wh . . . what friend?"

"Your director friend. Who was doing the ninety-minute special."

"It . . . uh . . ."

The room went silent.

"Or *was* there a friend?"

"Ask anybody in the business. I'm one of the best a.d.'s around."

"Did you go out there to work, Bandler? Or did you go out there with a dame?"

"I . . ."

"A dame," Meyer said, nodding.

"I'm telling you I loved Blanche. Why would I go to California with another woman?"

"Why, Bandler?" Hawes asked.

116

"I . . ."

"*Why,* Bandler?"

"I . . . *loved* . . . Blanche. I . . . what . . . what the hell was the harm of a little . . . a little innocent fun with . . . with somebody else? She . . . she knew I'd come back to her. She knew that girl meant nothing to me. She knew that."

"Apparently she didn't."

Bandler was silent for a long time. Then he said, "I saw it in the papers out there. Just a little item. About . . . about Blanche jump . . . jumping off that building. I saw it the day after she did it. I . . . I ditched the girl and got a plane back as fast as I could. Saturday. That was the earliest I could book. But she'd been buried by the time I got here and . . . and when I talked to the landlady of her building, she told me what she'd heard you say, so I . . . I figured you had it coming to you. For . . . for killing the girl I loved."

"You just go on believing that," Carella said.

"Huh?"

"It'll make the time pass more quickly."

"Huh?"

"You can get up to ten years for first-degree assault." Carella paused. "What was the harm of a little innocent fun, huh, Bandler?"

13

Love was in riotous bloom on the day that Fred Hassler came back to the squadroom and set the merry-go-round in violent motion once again. He had no idea he was reactivating the carousel, no knowledge that it had just about run down, or that the Tommy Barlow–Irene Thayer suicide was in danger of being thrown into the Open File. Police work is always a race against time, especially in a precinct like the 87th. A crime is committed, and the bulls go to work on it quickly and efficiently because anything that's likely to turn up is going to turn up *soon* or not at all. They'll go over the ground a hundred times, asking the same questions over and over again in hope of getting a different answer. But a case goes cold too quickly, and in a place like the 87th, there are always new cases, there is always a steady press of crime, there is always a fresh occurrence demanding investigation, there is always the Open File. The Open File is a convenience which allows cops to close a case while keeping it open. Once a case is dumped into the Open File, they can stop thinking about it, and concentrate instead on the three dozen other cases that have miraculously become a part of their working day routine. The case in the Open File is not officially closed since it hasn't officially been solved—there has been no arrest and conviction. But if it is not officially closed, neither is it truly active; it is simply laying there like a bagel. The Tommy Barlow–Irene Thayer case had lost all its momentum, and the cops of the 87th were almost ready to throw it into the Open File on the day Fred Hassler reappeared at the squadroom railing, on the day love was in riotous bloom.

The lovers were fifty-eight and fifty-five years old respectively, and they were standing before Detective Meyer's desk arguing heatedly. The man wore a sports jacket which he had thrown on over his undershirt when the arresting patrolman had knocked on the door. The woman wore a flowered house dress.

"All right, now who's pressing charges?" Meyer wanted to know.

"*I'm* pressing charges," the man and woman said together.

"One at a time."

"*I'm* pressing charges," the woman said.

"*I'm* pressing charges," the man said.

Hassler, standing at the slatted railing, tried to catch the attention of someone in the squadroom, but they all seemed to be busy filing or typing, except Meyer who was busy listening to the lovers.

"Who called the police?" Meyer asked.

"*I* called the police," the woman said.

"Is that true, sir?"

"Sure," the man said. "Big mouth called the police."

"All right, ma'am, why'd you call the police?"

"Because he pinched me," the woman said.

"Big mouth," the man said.

"Because he pinched you, huh?" Meyer asked patiently. "Are you married, folks?"

"We're married," the man said. "Big mouth can't stand a little pinch from her own husband. Right away, she has to yell cop."

"Shut up, you rotten animal," the woman said. "You grabbed a hunk, I thought you were gonna rip it off."

"I was being friendly."

"Some friendly."

"I should have been the one who called the cops," the man protested. "But I'm not a big mouth."

"You pinched me!" she insisted.

"Wash our dirty laundry," the man muttered. "Call the cops. Why didn't you call the F.B.I. already?"

"Let's try to calm down," Meyer said. "Lady, if your husband pinched you . . ."

"She hit me with a frying pan!" the man said suddenly.

"Ah!" the woman shouted. "Ah! Listen! Just listen!"

"That's right, she hit me with a . . ."

"And he calls *me* big mouth! Listen to him!"

"You hit me, Helen, it's the truth."

"You pinched me, and *that's* the truth!"

"I pinched you 'cause you hit me."

"I hit you 'cause you pinched me."

"Look, one at a time," Meyer warned. "Now what happened?"

"I was washing the dishes," the woman said. "He came up behind me and pinched me."

"Tell him, tell him," the man said, shaking his head. "Nothing sacred between a man and a wife. Blab it all to the police."

"Then what happened?"

119

"Then I took a frying pan from the sink, and I hit him with it."

"On the head," the man said. "You want to see what she done? Here, just feel this lump."

"Go ahead, tell him everything," the woman said.

"You were the one who called the police!" the man shouted.

"Because you threatened to kill me!"

"You hit me with the goddamn frying pan, didn't you?"

"You got me angry, that's why."

"From a little pinch?"

"It was a big pinch. I got a mark from it. You want to see the mark, officer?"

"Sure, go ahead, show him," the man said. "We'll make this a burlesque house. Go ahead, show him."

"How long have you been married?" Meyer asked patiently.

"Twenty-five years," the man said.

"Twenty-three years," the woman corrected.

"It seems more like twenty-five," the man said, and then burst out laughing at his own wit.

"In addition to beating his wife," the woman said, "he's also, as you can see, a comedian."

"I didn't beat you, I *pinched* you!"

"Why don't you both go home and patch it up?" Meyer asked.

"With him? With this rotten animal?"

"With her? With this loud mouth?"

"Come on, come on, it's springtime, the flowers are blooming, go home and kiss and make up," Meyer said. "We got enough troubles around here without having to lock you both up."

"Lock us up?" the man said indignantly. "For what? For a little love tap with a frying pan?"

"For a friendly pinch between husband and wife?" the woman asked.

"We *love* each other," the man protested.

"I know you do. So go on home, okay?" Meyer winked at the man. "Okay?"

"Well . . ."

"Sure," Meyer said, rising, scooping them both in his widespread arms, shoving them toward the gate in the railing. "Nice young couple like you shouldn't be wasting time arguing. Go on home, it's a beautiful day, how do you do, sir, can I help you?"

120

"My name's Fred Hassler," Hassler said. "I've been here before, but . . ."

"You mean we can just go?" the man asked.

"Yes," Meyer said, "go, go. Before I change my mind. Go on, scram." He turned to Hassler and said, "Yes, sir, I remember you now. Won't you come in? Don't pinch her any more, mister! And you lay off the frying pans. Have a seat, Mr. Hassler."

"Thank you," Hassler said. He did not seem very interested in the color or atmosphere of the squadroom this time. He seemed very serious, and a trifle angry, and Meyer wondered what had provoked his visit, and then called across the squadroom to where Carella was typing at his own desk.

"Steve, Mr. Hassler's here. You remember him, don't you?"

Carella got up from his desk, walked to where Hassler was sitting, and extended his hand. "Hello, Mr. Hassler, how are you?" he asked.

"Fine, thank you," Hassler said a bit brusquely.

"What can we do for you?" Meyer asked.

"You can get back my stuff," Hassler replied.

"What stuff?"

"I don't know if it was you or the Forty Thieves who took it, but somebody took it, and I want it back."

"Is something missing from your apartment, Mr. Hassler?" Carella asked.

"Yes, something is missing from my apartment. I'm not saying it was the police. It might have been the firemen. But . . ."

"You think the firemen took it?"

"I'm saying it's possible. They break into an apartment and next thing you know, everything is sticking to their fingers. Well, this time a citizen is complaining. A citizen has a right to complain, hasn't he?"

"Certainly, Mr. Hassler. What's missing?"

"To begin with, I'm a good sleeper."

"Yes, sir."

"Yes. I don't usually have trouble. But they've begun construction on our block, and last night they were making such a terrible racket that I went to the medicine chest to get some of these sleeping pills that I had one time when I had the flu, it must have been in nineteen fifty-nine."

"Yes, sir."

"Yes, I had this high fever, a hundred and two, almost a hundred and three, and I couldn't sleep, so I got these pills, they're called Barbinal, you take one and it knocks you out like

121

a light for the whole night. I had four of those pills left in a bottle from the time I had the flu in nineteen fifty-nine."

"Yes, sir?"

"Yes, well last night I couldn't sleep so I went to the medicine chest figuring I would take one of those Barbinals, and I found the bottle all right, but it was empty."

"The pills were gone?"

"All four of them. So I knew the firemen had been in the apartment at the time of the explosion, and I also knew the police had been crawling all over it, so I automatically figured. That was the first thing."

"Something else was missing, Mr. Hassler?"

"Mmmm," Hassler said grimly. "This morning, when I got up, I thought I'd just make a check of the apartment to see what else had been stolen. Well, a whole reel of film is missing."

"Film?"

"Movie film. I told you I was a bug on movies, I keep them all stored in my living room, the reels, in these metal containers, you know? And on the cover of each container, there's a strip of adhesive tape and it gives the date and tells what's on the reel. Well, a reel is missing."

"Perhaps you misplaced it, Mr. Hassler."

"I didn't misplace it. Those reels are all filed chronologically in a wooden case I made myself, with a space for each reel, and one of those spaces is empty. So, if you don't mind, I'd like my pills back, and also my film."

"We haven't got either, Mr. Hassler." Carella paused. "It's possible, you know, that Tommy and Irene took those pills. To put themselves to sleep."

"I thought they drank themselves to sleep."

"They may have taken the pills, Mr. Hassler."

"Did they take my film, too? They were both half-naked and dead, and my film wasn't anywhere on them. Besides, Tommy didn't like that particular reel."

"Tommy saw this reel?"

"Saw it? He was *in* it."

"What do you mean, Mr. Hassler?"

"I told you the first time I was up here that Tommy used to help me with my movies. I got this bug, you know, can I help it? So this one was the story of a guy who's broke, and he's walking in the park and he finds a hundred-dollar bill. So Tommy and I went over to Grover Park one afternoon, and we shot the whole thing, almost three hundred feet in one afternoon. There's only Tommy in it—no, wait a minute, there's also a little kid we found in the park and asked him to be in the picture. The way the plot goes, you see, Tommy finds this bill and then has to decide . . ."

"Tommy *acted* in this film, Mr. Hassler, is that right?"

"That's right." Hassler paused. "He wasn't a professional actor, you know, but what the hell, we were doing it for kicks, anyway. It came out pretty good." He shrugged. "Tommy didn't like it, though. He said he needed a haircut, and it made his face look too thin. Anyway, *I* liked it, and I want it back."

"But you see, we haven't got it," Carella said.

"Then the firemen must have it."

"Mr. Hassler, how was this reel of film labeled?"

"The usual way."

"Which is?"

"First the date on the top line. Then the title of the reel, which in this case was 'The Hundred Dollar Bill.' Then, after that it said 'with Tommy Barlow and Sammy La Paloma'— that's the name of the kid we discovered in the park. That's all."

"Then anyone who looked at the cover of the can would know that Tommy Barlow was in this reel of film."

"That's right."

"Mr. Hassler, thank you very much," Carella said. "We'll try our best to get it back for you."

"It was the Forty Thieves," Hassler insisted. "Those louses'll take the sink if it isn't nailed down."

But Carella wasn't at all sure the firemen were responsible for the theft of Fred Hassler's film. Carella was remembering that Mary Tomlinson had said, "I wish I had some pictures of Tommy, too. I have a lot of Margaret, but none of the man she was going to marry." And he was remembering that Michael Thayer had said, "I want to keep looking at him. That's strange, isn't it? I want to find out what was so . . . *different* about him." And he was remembering, too, that Amos Barlow had said, "Ever since he died, I've been going around the house looking for traces of him. Old letters, snapshots, anything that was Tommy." So whereas he knew that perhaps the firemen had earned their nickname with good reason, he also knew that none of the Forty Thieves would be crazy enough to steal a container of home movies. The carousel music had suddenly started again. The gold ring was once more in sight. The horses were in motion.

Carella went downtown and swore out three search warrants.

Hawes, in the meantime, perhaps motivated by the sudden burst of activity on the case, decided that he wanted to talk to Miss Martha Tamid one more time. They were each, Carella and Hawes, about to gasp their last breath on this case, but they were nonetheless still giving it the old college try. Hawes didn't really believe that Martha Tamid had anything at all to do with the suicide-homicide, but there remained nonetheless the fact that she had lied about going to Amos Barlow's house on the afternoon of April 16. The specific purpose of his visit was to find out why she had lied. She told him immediately and without hesitation.

"Because I was embarrassed."

"Embarrassed, Miss Tamid?"

"Yes, how would you feel? I knew he was in there. I could see his car in the garage. But he wouldn't answer the doorbell. Well, no matter. It is finished."

"What do you mean, finished? No, don't answer that yet, Miss Tamid, we'll come back to it. I want to get something else straight first. You're saying that you lied to the police because your feelings were hurt? Is that what you're telling me?"

"Yes."

"Suppose you tell me why you went there in the first place, Miss Tamid?"

"You are getting harsh with me," Martha said, her eyes seeming to get larger and a little moist.

"I'm terribly sorry," Hawes answered. "Why did you go there?"

Martha Tamid shrugged. "Because I do not like being ignored," she said. "I am a woman."

"Why did you go there, Miss Tamid?"

"To make love," she answered simply.

Hawes was silent for several moments. Then he said, "But Amos Barlow wouldn't open the door."

"He would not. Of course, he did not know why I was coming there."

"Otherwise he most certainly *would* have opened the door, is that right?"

"No, he would not have opened the door, anyway. I know that now. But I thought I would mention to you, anyway, that he did not know I was coming to make love."

"Are you in love with Amos Barlow?" Hawes asked.

"Don't be ridiculous!"

"*Were* you in love with him?"

"Certainly not!"

"But you nonetheless went there that Sunday to . . . to seduce him?"

"Yes."

"Why?"

"Because I am a woman."

"Yes, you've already told me that."

"I do not like to be ignored."

"You've told me that, too."

"Then? It's simple, *n'est-ce pas?*" She nodded emphatically. "Besides, it's finished now. I no longer care."

"Why is it finished, Miss Tamid? Why do you no longer care?"

"Because he was here, and now I know, and now I do not feel unattractive anymore."

"When was he here?"

"Four nights ago, five nights? I don't remember exactly."

"He came of his own accord?"

"I invited him."

"And? What happened?"

"Nothing."

"Nothing?"

"Nothing." Martha nodded. "I am a very patient woman, you know. My patience is endless. But, you know . . . I gave him every opportunity. He is simply . . . he is inexperienced . . . he knows *nothing,* but nothing. And there is a limit to anyone's patience."

"I'm not sure I follow you, Miss Tamid," Hawes said.

"You cannot blame a person for being inexperienced. This is not the same thing as being inattentive, you know. So when I tried, and I realized he was . . . *comment dit-on?* . . . simple? naïf? ingénu? . . . what is there to do? He did not know. He simply did not know."

"What didn't he know, Miss Tamid?"

"What to do, how to do! He did not know." She leaned forward suddenly. "I can trust you, can't I? You are like a *confesseur,* sin't that true? A priest who hears confession? I can tell you?"

"Sure," Hawes said.

"I took off my own blouse," Martha said, "because he was fumbling so with the buttons. But then . . . he did not know how to undress me. He simply did not know. He had never been with a woman before, do you understand? He is an innocent." Martha Tamid sat back in her chair. "One cannot be offended by innocence," she said.

The police who went through all those rooms were pretty much offended by all the rampant innocence. They searched Mary Tomlinson's house from basement to attic, and they went through every inch of Michael Thayer's apartment, and they covered Amos Barlow's house like a horde of termites—but they didn't turn up hide or hair of the film that had been stolen from Fred Hassler. They went through Mrs. Tomlinson's tiny little Volkswagen, and through Michael Thayer's blue Oldsmobile sedan, and through Amos Barlow's tan Chevrolet, but they found nothing. They searched through Thayer's small office in the Brio Building, and through Barlow's mailing room at 891 Mayfair—but they did not find the film, and the merry-go-round was slowing to a halt again.

The next day, without realizing how close they'd come to grabbing the gold ring, the detectives held a meeting in the squadroom.

"What do you think?" Hawes asked. "Have you got any ideas?"

"None," Carella said.

"Meyer?"

Meyer shook his head.

"Bert?"

Kling hesitated a moment, and then said, "No."

"So do we call it a suicide and close it out?" Hawes asked.

"What the hell else can we do?" Meyer asked.

"Let's ask Pete for permission to leave it in the Open File," Carella said.

"That's the same thing as killing it," Hawes said.

Carella shrugged. "Something may come up on it some day."

"When?"

"Who knows? We've run it into the ground. What else can we do?"

Hawes hesitated, unwilling to be the one who officially killed the case. "You want to vote on it?" he asked. The detectives nodded. "All those in favor of asking Pete to dump it in Siberia?" None of the men raised their hands.

"Meyer?"

"Dump it," Meyer said.

"Bert?"

"Dump it."

"Steve?"

Carella paused for a long time. Then he nodded reluctantly and said, "Dump it. Dump it."

126

The request was placed on Lieutenant Peter Byrnes' desk that afternoon. He glanced at it cursorily, picked up his pen, and then signed it, granting his permission. Before he went home that night, Alf Miscolo, filing a sheaf of papers he'd picked up from all the desks in the squadroom, went to the green cabinet marked OPEN FILE, slid out the drawer and dropped into it a manila folder containing all the papers on the Tommy Barlow–Irene Thayer case.

For all intents and purposes, the case was closed.

14

The man was lying on his back in Grover Park.

They had already traced the outline of his body on the moist grass by the time Carella and Hawes arrived, and the man seemed ludicrously framed by his own ridiculous posture, the white powder capturing the position of death and freezing it. The police photographer was performing his macabre dance around the corpse, choreographing himself into new angles each time his flash bulb popped. The corpse stared up at him unblinkingly, twisted into the foolish grotesquery of death, one leg bent impossibly beneath him, the other stretched out straight. The sun was shining. It was May, and there was the heady aroma of newly mown grass in the park, the delicious fragrance of magnolia and cornelian cherry and quince. The man had a knife in his heart.

They stood around the body exchanging the amenities, men who were called together only when Death gave a party. The lab boys, the photographer, the assistant medical examiner, the two detectives from Homicide North, the two men from the 87th, they all stood around the man with the knife sticking out of his chest, and they asked each other how they were, and had they heard about Manulus over in the 33rd, got shot by a burglar night before last, what about this moonlighting stuff, did they think the commissioner would stick to his guns, it was a nice day, wasn't it, beautiful weather they'd been having this spring, hardly a drop of rain. They cracked a few jokes—the photographer had one about the first astronaut to reach the moon—and they went about their work with a faintly detached air of busyness. That was a dead man lying in the grass there. They accepted his presence only by performing a mental sleight of hand that in effect denied his humanity. He was no longer a man, he was simply a problem.

Carella pulled the knife from the dead man's chest as soon as the assistant m.e. and the photographer were through with the stiff, carefully lifting the knife with his handkerchief tented over his hand, so as not to smear any latent prints that might be on the handle or blade.

"You going to make out the tag?" one of the laboratory boys asked him.

"Yeah," Carella answered curtly.

He pulled three or four evidence tags from his back pocket, slid one loose from the rubber-banded stack, returned the others to his pocket, took the cap from his fountain pen, and began writing:

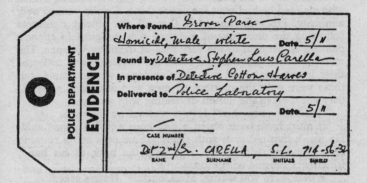

Automatically, he turned over the tag and filled in the information requested on the reverse side:

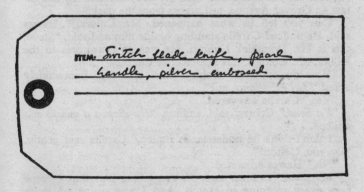

He looped the strings of the tag over the handle of the knife, fastening the two together where blade joined handle. Then, carrying the knife by the tag, he went over to where the laboratory technician was making a sketch of the body and its location.

"Might as well take this with you," Carella said.

"Thanks," the technician said. He accepted the knife and carried it over to his car which was parked partly on the grass, partly on the road that wound through the park. An ambulance had already arrived, and the attendants were waiting for everyone to finish with the body so they could cart it off to the morgue for autopsy. Hawes, standing some ten feet from where the attendants waited, was questioning a man who claimed he had seen the entire thing. Carella walked over aimlessly. He sometimes felt that all the official rigmarole following the discovery of a corpse was designed to allow a painless adjustment to the very idea of death by violence. The men took their pictures and made their sketches and collected their latent prints and whatever evidence was available, but these were only the motions of men who were stalling while they got used to the notion of dealing with a corpse.

"What time was this?" Hawes was asking the man.

"It must have been about a half-hour ago," the man said. He was a thin old man with rheumy blue eyes and a running nose. He kept wiping his nose with the back of his hand, which was crusted with mucus.

"Where were you sitting, Mr. Coluzzi?" Hawes asked.

"Right there on that high rock. I was making a drawing of the lake. I come here every morning, and I sketch a little. I'm retired, you see. I live with my daughter and my son-in-law on Grover Avenue, just across from the park."

"Can you tell us what happened, Mr. Coluzzi?" Hawes said. He noticed Carella standing beside him and said, "Steve, this is Mr. Dominick Coluzzi. He was an eyewitness to the killing. Mr. Coluzzi, this is Detective Carella."

"How do you do?" Coluzzi said, and then immediately asked, *"Lei è Italiano, no?"*

"Yes," Carella answered.

"Va bene," Coluzzi said, smiling. *"Ho dicevo a questo suo amico . . ."*

"I don't think he understands Italian," Carella said gently. "Do you, Cotton?"

"No," Hawes answered.

"Mi scusi," Coluzzi said. "I was telling him that I come here every morning to sketch. And I was sitting up there when the car pulled up."

"What kind of a car was it, Mr. Coluzzi?" Carella asked.

"A Cadillac convertible," Coluzzi said without hesitation.

"The color?"

"Blue."

"Top up or down?"

"Up."

"You didn't happen to notice the license plate number, did you?"

"I did," Coluzzi said, and he wiped his nose with the back of his hand. "I wrote it down on my pad."

"You're a very observant person, Mr. Coluzzi," Hawes said, his brows raised in admiration.

Coluzzi shrugged and wiped his nose with the back of his hand. "It isn't every day you see a man get stabbed to death," he said. He was plainly enjoying himself. He was perhaps sixty-seven, sixty-eight, a thin old man whose arms were still muscular and wiry, but whose hands trembled slightly, a thin old man who had been let out to pasture, who came to the park each morning to sketch. This morning which had started out the way all other mornings did for him, something new had come into his life. He had been watching the lake and sketching the section near the dock where the rowboats bobbed in imperfect unison when suddenly a Cadillac had pulled to the side of the winding road, and suddenly murder had been done. And the old man, unnoticed on his high boulder overlooking the lake and the scene of the murder, alert, quick, and watched, and then shouted at the killer, and then had written down the number of the car's license plate as it drove away. For the first time in a long time, the old man was useful again, and he enjoyed his usefulness, enjoyed talking to these two men who admired his quick thinking, who spoke to him as if they were speaking to an equal, as if they were speaking to another *man*, and not to some child who had to be let out into the sunshine each morning.

"What was the number of the plate, Mr. Coluzzi?" Carella asked.

Coluzzi opened his sketch pad. He had been working in charcoal, and a delicately shaded drawing of the boats at the dock filled half of the page. In one corner of the page, in charcoal, he had written:

$$IS-7146$$

Carella noticed that he had crossed the seven, in the Continental manner. He nodded briefly to himself, and then copied the number into his own pad.

"Can you tell us exactly what happened, Mr. Coluzzi?" he said.

"The car pulled to the curb. Down there." Coluzzi pointed. "I noticed it right away because it came in with a lot of noise, tires shrieking, door slamming. And then a man ran up the embankment directly to this other man who was sitting on the bench there. The other man got up right away, and tried to run, but the one who got out of the car was too fast for him. He caught his arm and swung him around, and then he brought his right hand around and at first I thought he was only punching him, do you know, with his right hand, but instead he was stabbing him. I stood up on the rock and yelled at him, and that was when he turned and looked at me, and began running down to the car again. I think he was frightened. I don't think he would have left his knife sticking in the man that way, if he hadn't been frightened."

"Are *you* frightened, Mr. Coluzzi?"

"Me? Of what?"

"Of telling us all this? Of possible reprisal?"

"Reprisal? What's that?"

"*Vendetta*," Carella said in Italian.

"*Ma che cosa?*" the old man said. "*Vendetta? Che importa?* I'm an old man. What are they going to do with their *vendetta*? Kill me? If this is the worst that can happen to me, I welcome it."

"We appreciate your help, Mr. Coluzzi."

"The way I figure it, a man is entitled in this country to come to the park and sit on a bench if he wants to. No one has the right to murder him while he is sitting on a bench minding his own business."

"Thanks again," Carella said.

"*Prego*," the old man answered, and went back to sketching the rowboats on the lake.

The old man's eyesight was good, even though he was sixty-seven years old. A call to the Bureau of Motor Vehicles confirmed that a blue 1960 Cadillac convertible bearing the license plate IS-7146 was registered to a Mr. Frank Dumas at 1137 Fairview in, of course, Isola. The "IS" on the plate made the Isola address mandatory. Carella thanked the clerk at the bureau, turned to Hawes, and said, "Too easy. It's too damn easy."

Hawes shrugged and answered, "We haven't got him yet."

They checked out a sedan and drove downtown to Fairview Street. Carella was thinking that he had drawn Lineup the next day, and that would mean getting up an hour earlier in order to be all the way downtown on time. Hawes was thinking that he was due in court on Monday to testify in a burglary case. They drove with the windows in the car open. The car was an old Buick, fitted with a police radio and new tires. It had been a good car in its day, but Carella wondered what it would do in a chase with one of this year's souped-up models. Fairview Street was thronged with people who had come outdoors simply to talk to each other or to catch a breath of spring air. They parked the car at the curb in front of 1137, and began walking toward the building. The people on the front stoop knew immediately that they were cops. The sedan was unmarked, and both Carella and Hawes were wearing business suits, and shirts and ties, but the people sitting on the front stoop of the tenement knew they were cops and would have known it even if they'd walked up those steps wearing Bermuda shorts and sneakers. A cop has a smell. If you live long enough in an area infested with cops, you get to know the smell. You get to fear it, too, because cops are one thing you can never figure. They will help you one moment and turn on you the next. The people sitting on the front stoop watched Carella and Hawes, two strangers, mount the front steps and walk into the vestibule. The stoop cleared immediately. The two young men standing there immediately decided to go to the candy store for an egg cream. The old man from the building next door decided to go up on the roof and look at his pigeons. The old lady who lived on the ground floor packed up her knitting, picked up her folding chair, and went inside to watch daytime television. Cops almost always spelled trouble, and detectives spelled the biggest kind of trouble.

Carella and Hawes, not unaware of the subtle discrimination taking place behind them, studied the mailboxes and found a listing for Mr. Frank Dumas in apartment 44. They went through the vestibule and up the steps. On the second floor, they passed a little girl who was sitting on the steps tightening her skates with a skate key.

"Hello," she said.

"Hello," Carella answered.

"Are you coming to my house?" she asked.

"Where's your house?"

"A pommin twenny-one."

"No, sorry," Carella said, smiling.

"I thought you was the insurance," the little girl said, and went back to tightening her skates.

On the fourth-floor landing, they drew their guns. Apartment 44 was in the middle of the hall. They walked silently to the door, listened outside for a moment, and then flanked it. Carella nodded at Hawes who braced himself for a flat-footed kick at the lock.

He was bringing back his knee when the shots came from within the apartment, shockingly loud, splintering the door.

15

Hawes dropped at the sound of the first shot, just as the splintered hole appeared in the wooden door. The slug whistled past his head as he fell flat to the floor, and then ricocheted off the wall behind him and went caroming at a crazy angle down the hallway just as the second shot erupted. The wood splintered again, and Carella winced as the slug tore its way across the narrow corridor, inches from his face where he stood to the left of the door, his gun pulled in tight against his chest, his head pulled down into his shoulders. On the floor, Hawes was scrambling away to the right of the door as the third shot came. The next four shots followed almost immediately, ripping wood from the door, ricocheting, into the cracked ceiling overhead. He had counted seven shots, an empty automatic if the person inside was firing a certain type of .45. There was a pause. The man could be reloading. Or he could be firing another type of .45 with a magazine capacity of nine cartridges, or a Harrington & Richardson .22 with the same capacity, or . . . there was no time to run through a gun catalogue. He could be reloading, or simply waiting, or even carrying two guns—or he could at this moment be climbing out the window. Carella took a deep breath. He backed off across the hallway, braced himself against the opposite wall, and unleashed the sole of his foot at the lock on the door.

The door sprang inward, and Carella followed it into a hail of bullets that came from the window. Hawes was immediately behind him. They both dropped flat to the worn linoleum inside the apartment, firing at the window where the figure of a man appeared in silhouette for just a moment, and then vanished. They got to their feet, and rushed across the room. Carella put his head outside the window, and then pulled it back at once as a shot sounded somewhere above him, and a piece of red brick spattered against his cheek.

"He's heading for the roof!" he shouted to Hawes, not turning to look, knowing that Hawes would take the steps up, and knowing that he himself would climb onto the fire escape in pursuit within the next few moments. He reloaded his gun from the cartridge belt at his waist, and then stepped out onto the fire escape. He fired a quick shot at the figure two stories above him, and then began clambering up the iron-runged steps. The man above did not fire again. Instead, as he climbed, he began dropping a barrage of junk collected from the fire escapes he passed: flower pots, an iron, a child's toy truck, an old and battered suitcase, all of which crashed around Carella as he made his way steadily up each successive ladder. The barrage stopped when the man gained the roof. Three shots echoed on the still spring air. Hawes had reached the roof.

By the time Carella joined him, the man had leaped the area-way between the two buildings and was out of sight.

"He got away while I was reloading," Hawes said.

Carella nodded, and then holstered his .38.

When they got back to the squad room, Meyer was waiting with a report on Frank Dumas.

"No record," he said, "not in this city, at least. I'm waiting for word from the Feds."

"That's too bad," Carella said. "It looked like a professional job."

"Maybe he *is* a pro."

"You just said he had no record."

"How do we know Dumas is his right name?"

"The car was registered . . ."

"I talked to MVB a little more," Meyer said. "The car was registered only last month. He could have used an alias."

"That wouldn't have tied with his driver's license."

"Since when do thieves worry about driver's licenses?"

"Thieves are the most careful drivers in the world," Carella said.

"I also checked the phone book. There are six listings for Frank Dumas. I'll bet you next month's salary against a bagel that Dumas is an alias he picked right out of the directory."

"Maybe."

"It's worth checking," Meyer told them.

He also told Carella and Hawes that Detective Andy Parker's surveillance of a suspected shooting gallery would be paid off this evening at 7:00 P.M. The lieutenant needed five men for the raid, and the names of Carella and Hawes were on the list. "We're mustering here at six-thirty," Meyer said.

"I'd planned to go home at six," Carella answered.

"The best laid plans," Meyer said, "aft get screwed up."

"Yeah." Carella scratched his head. "What do you want

to do, Cotton? Go back to Fairview and talk to the landlady or somebody?"

"She ought to know who rented that apartment," Hawes said.

"You had lunch yet?" Meyer asked.

"No."

"Get something to eat first. The landlady'll wait."

They had lunch in a diner near the precinct. Carella was wondering whether the lab would come up with anything positive on that switchblade knife. He was also wondering why the killer had chosen to use a knife in the park when he obviously owned at least one gun.

"Do you think he saw us pulling up downstairs?" Carella asked.

"He must have. The way that stoop cleared, he'd have had to be an idiot not to know we were cops."

"This doughnut is stale," Carella said. "How's yours?"

"It's all right. Here, take half of it."

"No, go ahead."

"I won't be able to finish it, anyway."

"Thanks," Carella said. He sliced Hawes' doughnut in half and began munching on it. "That's better," he said. He looked at his watch. "We'd better get moving. He's got a head start on us already. If we can at least find out whether Dumas is his real name . . ."

"Just let me finish my tea," Hawes said.

The landlady at 1137 Fairview Street wasn't happy to see cops, and she told them so immediately.

"There's always cops here," she said. "I'm fed up to here with cops."

"That's too bad, lady," Hawes said, "but we've got to ask you some questions, anyway."

"You always come around shooting, and then you ask the questions later," the landlady said angrily.

"Lady, the man in apartment 44 began shooting first," Hawes said.

"That's *your* story."

"Who was he, do you know?"

"Who's going to pay for all that damage to the hallway, can you tell me that?"

"Not us," Hawes said flatly. "What's the man's name?"

"John Doe."

"Come on, lady."

"That's his name. That's the name he took the apartment under."

137

"How long has he been living here?"

"Two months."

"Did he pay his rent in cash or by check?"

"Cash."

"Didn't you suspect John Doe might not be his real name? Especially since the name Frank Dumas is on his mailbox?"

"I'm not a cop," the landlady said. "It's not my job to *suspect* somebody who comes here to rent an apartment. He paid me a month in advance, and he didn't holler about the increase over the last tenant, or the four dollars for the television aerial, so why should I suspect him? I don't care if his name's John Doe or John D. Rockefeller, so long as he pays the rent and doesn't cause trouble."

"But he's caused a little trouble, hasn't he?"

"*You're* the ones caused the trouble," the landlady said. "Coming here with your guns and shooting up the hallway. Do you know there was a little girl sitting on the steps while you were shooting? Do you know that?"

"The little girl was on the second floor, ma'am," Carella said. "And besides, we didn't expect shooting."

"Then you don't know cops the way I do. The minute a cop arrives, there's shooting."

"We'd like to go through Mr. Doe's apartment," Carella said.

"Then you'd better go get yourself a search warrant."

"Come on, lady, break your heart," Hawes said. "You don't want us to go all the way downtown, do you?"

"I don't care where you go. If you want to search that apartment, you need a warrant. That's the law."

"You know, of course, that your garbage cans are still outside on the sidewalk, don't you?" Carella said.

"Huh?"

"Your garbage cans. They're supposed to be taken in by noon. It's one-thirty now."

"I'll take them in right away," the landlady said. "The damn trucks didn't *get* here until noon."

"That's unfortunate," Carella said, "but taking them in now won't change the nature of the misdemeanor. There's a stiff fine involved, you know."

"What is this? A shakedown?"

"That's exactly what it is, lady," Hawes said. "You don't *really* want us to go all the way downtown for a search warrant, do you?"

"Cops," the landlady muttered, and she turned her back.

"Go ahead, look through the apartment. Try not to steal anything while you're up there."

"We'll try," Carella said, "but it won't be easy."

They began climbing the steps to the fourth floor. The same little girl was sitting on the second floor landing, still adjusting her skates with the skate key.

"Hello," she said.

"Hello," Carella answered.

"Are you coming to my house?"

"Apartment twenty-one?" Carella asked.

"That's right."

"No, I'm sorry."

"I thought you was the insurance," the little girl said, and went back to work on the skate.

The door to apartment 44 was open when they reached the fourth floor landing. Carella's kick had sprung the lock, and the door stood ajar, knifing a wedge of sunlight into the otherwise dark hallway. They walked to the door and casually shoved it open.

A young woman turned swiftly from the dresser where she was going through the drawers. She was perhaps eighteen years old, her hair in curlers, wearing neither make-up nor lipstick, a faded pink robe thrown over her pajamas.

"Well, hello," Carella said.

The girl pulled a face, as if she were four years old and had been caught doing something that was strictly forbidden by her parents.

"You're cops, huh?" she said.

"That's right," Hawes answered. "What are you doing here, miss?"

"Looking around, that's all."

"Just browsing, huh?" Carella said.

"Well, sort of, yes."

"What's your name?"

"Cynthia."

"Cynthia what?"

"I didn't take anything, mister," Cynthia said. "I just came in to look around, that's all. I live right down the hall. You can ask anybody."

"What do you want us to ask them?"

"If I don't live right down the hall."

Cynthia shrugged. Her face was getting more and more discouraged, crumbling slowly, the way a very little girl's face will steadily dissolve under the questioning of adults.

"What's your last name, Cynthia?"

"Reilly," she said.

"What are you doing in here, Cynthia?"

Cynthia shrugged.

"Stealing?"

"No!" she said. "Hey, no! No, I swear to God."

"Then what?"

"Just looking around."

"Do you know the man who lives in this apartment?"

"No. I only saw him in the hall once or twice."

"Do you know his name?"

"No." Cynthia paused. "I'm sick," she said. "I've got a bad cold. That's why I'm in my bathrobe. I couldn't go to work because I had a fever of a hundred and one point six."

"So you decided to take a little walk, is that it?"

"Yes, that's it," Cynthia said. She smiled because she thought at last the detectives were beginning to understand what she was doing in this apartment, but the detectives didn't smile back, and her face returned to its slow crumbling, as if she were ready to burst into tears at any moment.

"And you walked right in here, huh?"

"Only because I was curious."

"About what?"

"The shooting." She shrugged. "Are you going to arrest me? I didn't take anything. I'll die if you take me to prison." She paused and then blurted, "I've got a fever."

"Then you better get back to bed," Carella said.

"You're letting me go?"

"Go on, get out of here."

"Thanks," Cynthia said quickly, and then vanished before they had a chance to change their minds.

Carella sighed. "You want to take this room? I'll get the other."

"Okay," Hawes said. Carella went into the other room. Hawes began looking through the dresser Cynthia had already inspected. He was working on the second drawer when he heard the sound of roller skates in the hallway outside. He looked up as the little girl from the second floor landing skated into the room.

"Hello," she said.

"Hello," Hawes answered.

"Did you just move in?"

"No."

"Are you going someplace?"

"No."

"Then why are you taking all your clothes out of the bureau?"

"They're not my clothes," Hawes said.

"Then you shouldn't be doing that."

"I guess not."

"Then why are you?"

"Because I'm trying to find something."

"What are you trying to find?"

"I'm trying to find the name of the man who lives in this apartment."

"Oh," the little girl said. She skated to the other side of the room, skated back, and then asked, "Is his name in the bureau?"

"Not so far," Hawes said.

"Do you think his name is in the bureau?"

"It might be. Here, do you see this?"

"It's a shirt," the little girl said.

"That's right, but I mean here, inside the collar."

"Those are numbers," the little girl said. "I can count to a hundred by tens, would you like to hear me?"

"Not right now," Hawes said. "Those numbers are a laundry mark," Hawes said. "We may be able to get the man's name by checking them out."

"Gee," the girl said and then immediately said, "Ten, twenty, thirty, fifty . . ."

"Forty," Hawes corrrected.

". . . *forty*, fifty, sixty, thirty . . ."

"Seventy."

"I better start all over again. Ten, twenty . . ." She stopped and studied Hawes carefully for a moment. Then she said, "You don't live here, do you?"

"No."

"I thought you did at first. I thought maybe you just moved in or something."

"No."

"I thought maybe Petie had moved out."

"No," Hawes said. He put a pile of shirts onto the dresser and then reached into his back pocket for a tag.

"Why do you need a laundry mark to tell you what Petie's name is?" the little girl asked.

"Because that's the only way we . . ." Hawes paused. "What did you say, honey?"

"I don't know. What did I say?"

"Something about . . . Petie?"

"Oh, yeah, Petie."

141

"Is that his name?"

"Whose name?"

"The man who lives here," Hawes said.

"I don't know. What does it say inside his shirts?"

"Well, never mind his shirts, honey. If you know his name, you can save us a lot of time."

"Are you a bull?" the little girl asked.

"Now what makes you ask that?"

"My poppa says bulls stink."

"Is Petie your poppa?"

The little girl began laughing. "Petie? My poppa is Dave, that's who my poppa is."

"Well . . . well, what about Petie?"

"What *about* Petie?"

"Is *that* his name?"

"I guess so. If that's what it says inside the shirts, then that must be his name."

"Petie what?"

"What Petie what?"

"His second name. Petie what?"

"Peter Piper picked a peck of pickled peppers," the girl said, and she began giggling. "Do you know how to skate?"

"Yes. Honey, what's Petie's second name?"

"I don't know. *My* second name is Jane. Alice Jane Horowitz."

"Did he ever *tell* you his second name?"

"Nooooo," the girl said, drawing out the word cautiously.

"How do you know his first name?"

"Because he showed me how to use a skate key."

"Yeah? Go ahead."

"That's all. I was sitting on the steps, and the skate wouldn't open, and he was coming downstairs, and he said, 'Here, Petie'll fix that for you,' and then he fixed it, so that's how I know his name is Petie."

"Thanks," Hawes said.

The little girl studied him solemnly for a moment and then said, "You *are* a bull, aren't you?"

The six bulls who met in the squadroom that night after dinner were not in the mood for a raid on a shooting gallery. Carella and Meyer wanted to be home with their wives and children. Andy Parker had been trying to get to a movie for the past week, but instead he'd been involved in this surveillance. Bert Kling wanted to finish a book he was reading. Cotton Hawes wanted to be with Christine Maxwell. Lieutenant Byrnes had promised his wife he'd take her to visit her cousin in Bethtown. But nonetheless, the six detectives met in the squadroom and were briefed by Parker on the location and setup of the apartment he'd had under surveillance for the past three weeks.

"They're shooting up in there, that's for sure," Parker said. "But I think something unusual happened last night. A guy came with a suitcase for the first time since I've been on the plant. And he left without it. I think a big delivery was made, and if we hit them tonight, we may be able to nab them with the junk."

"It's worth a try," Byrnes said. "The least we'll net is a few hopheads."

"Who'll be out on the street again by tomorrow," Carella said.

"Depending on how much they're holding," Hawes said.

"Someday, this city is going to get some realistic laws about narcotics," Carella said.

"*Aluvai,*" Meyer put in.

"Let's get moving," Byrnes said.

They traveled in one sedan because they wanted to arrive together, wanted to get out of the car and hit the apartment before the telegraphing grapevine was able to warn of the presence of cops in the neighborhood. As it was, their margin was a close one. The instant they pulled up in front of the tenement, a man sitting on the front stoop ran inside. Parker ran after him into the hallway and collared the man as he was knocking on a ground floor door. Parker hit him only once and without hesitation, a sharp rabbit punch at the base of the man's neck.

"Who's there?" somebody inside the apartment called.

"Me," Parker said, and by that time the other five detectives were in the hallway.

"Who's me?" the voice inside said, and Parker kicked in the door.

Nobody was shooting up that night. The apartment may have been filled with addicts on the other nights of Parker's surveillance, but tonight there was only a fat old man in an undershirt, a fat old woman in a house dress, and a young kid in a T shirt and dungarees. The trio was standing at the kitchen table, and they were working over what seemed to be eight million pounds of pure heroin. They were cutting it with sugar, diluting the junk for later sale to addicts from here to San Francisco and back again. The old man reached for a Luger in the drawer of the table the moment the door burst inward. He changed his mind about firing the gun because he was suddenly looking at an army of cops armed with everything from riot guns to Thompsons.

"Surprise!" Parker said, and the old man answered, "Drop dead, you cop bastard."

Parker, naturally, hit him.

The men got back to the squadroom at about eight-thirty. They all had coffee together, and then Cotton Hawes drove uptown to Christine Maxwell's apartment.

16

He loved to watch her strip. He told himself that all he was, after all, was a tired businessman who couldn't afford the price of a musical comedy on his meagre salary, who chose to watch Christine Maxwell rather than a stageful of chorus girls—but he knew he was not the ordinary *voyeur*, knew there was something rather more personal in his joy. He *was* tired, true, and perhaps he *was* only a businessman whose business happened to be crime and punishment. But sitting on the couch across the room from her, a glass of Scotch in his big hands, his bare feet resting on a throw pillow, he watched Christine as she took off her blouse, and he felt something more than simple anticipation. He wanted to hold her naked in his arms, wanted to make love to her, but she was more to him than a promised bed partner; she provided for him a haven, she was someone to whom he returned at the end of a long and difficult day, someone he was always happy to see and who, in turn, always made him feel welcome and wanted.

She reached behind her now and unclasped her brassière, releasing the full globes of her breasts, and then carrying the bra to the chair over whose back she had draped the blouse. She folded the bra in two over the blouse, unzipped her skirt and stepped out of it, folded that onto the seat of the chair, and then stepped out of her half slip and put that on top of the skirt. She took off her black, high-heeled pumps and put them to one side of the chair, and then ungartered her stockings, rolled them off her legs, and put those on the chair. too. She smiled unselfconsciously at him in the dimness of the room, removed her panties, threw them onto the chair and and then, wearing only her garter belt, walked to where he was stretched out on the couch.

"Take that off, too," he said.

"No," she said. "I like to leave something for you."

"Why?"

"I don't know." She grinned and kissed him on the mouth. "I don't like to make it too easy." She kissed him again. "What'd you do today?"

"Shot it out with a killer," he said.

"Did you get him?"

"No."

"Then what?"

"Went back to talk to his landlady."

"Any help?"

"Not much. A little girl gave us the guy's first name, though."

"Good."

"Petie," he said. "How many Peties do you think there are in this city?"

"Two million, I would suspect."

"Your mouth is nice tonight," he said, and he kissed her again.

"Mmmm."

"We went on a dope raid just before I came here. Got a whole suitcase of the stuff, about forty pounds of it, worth something like twelve million bucks."

"Did you bring some with you?"

"I didn't know you were a junkie," Hawes murmured.

"I'm a *secret* junkie," Christine whispered in his ear. "That's the worst kind."

"I know." He paused, grinning in the darkness. "I've got a few sticks of marijuana in my desk at the office. I'll bring them next time I come."

"Marijuana," Christine said. "That's kid stuff."

"You're on heroin, huh?"

"Absolutely." She bit his ear and then said, "Maybe we can work out something here. You must go on a lot of those raids, don't you?"

"Every now and then. Usually, we leave them to the Narcotics Squad."

"But you *do* get a certain amount of heroin, don't you?"

"Sure," Hawes said.

"Maybe we can trade," Christine said.

"Maybe." He kissed her on the neck and said, "Take off your pants."

"My pants *are* off," she answered.

"Your thing then, your garter belt."

"You do it."

He pulled her to him, his hands going behind her back to the clasps on the flimsy garment. He frowned suddenly and said, "Now, what the hell?"

"Yes?"

"I thought of something."

"What?"

"I don't know. It went in my mind, and then right out again. That's funny, isn't it?"

"Do you want me to help you with that?"

"No, I can do it." He frowned again. "That's funny, I . . . what are you doing with this thing on, anyway?"

"What?" Christine said, puzzled.

"Well, how . . . ?" He shook his head, "Never mind," he said, and he unclasped the garter belt and threw it across the room at the chair, missing.

"Now it's on the floor," Christine said.

"You want me to go pick it up?"

"No. You stay right here."

She kissed him, but his mouth was tight and she touched his face in the darkness and felt the frown still there, covering it like a mask.

"What is it?" she asked.

"Must be that guy today. Petie. Whatever his name is."

"What about him?"

"I don't know." He hesitated. "Something . . . I just . . . maybe not him. Something, though."

"Something about what?"

"I don't *know*. But something just . . . just popped into my mind, and I thought all at once, *Of course!* And then the thing went away and . . . something . . . something with murder."

"Then it *must* be that man today. The one you were shooting at."

"Sure, it must be, but . . ." He shook his head. "I'll be damned, to just run out of my mind like that." He pulled her close and kissed her throat, and then ran his hand down her thigh and then sat up suddenly and said, "The . . . the . . . the . . ."

"What?" she said. "What is it?"

"What do you take off?" he blurted.

"What?"

"Come on, Christine!" he said angrily, wanting her to understand immediately, and annoyed when she did not.

"What *is* it?"

"*First!*" he said. "What do you take off *first?*"

"When? What are you . . . ?"

"Does anybody wear pants *under* a garter belt? Does any woman?"

"Well, no, how could they?"

"Then how the hell . . . ?"

147

"Unless . . . well, I suppose . . ."

"Unless what?"

"Unless the panties were very brief. But still, it would be terribly awkward, Cotton. I don't see why any woman would . . ."

"They weren't!"

"What?"

"Brief. They weren't. And, damnit, the garter belt was on the chair!"

"What garter belt? It's on the floor, Cotton. You just threw it there yourself a few min . . ."

"Not yours! Irene's!" he shouted, and he rose from the couch suddenly.

"Who?"

"Irene Thayer! Her garter belt was on that chair with the rest of her clothes, but she was wearing her pants, Christine! Now how the hell did she manage that?"

"The suicide, do you mean? The one you were working on last month?"

"Suicide, my foot! How'd she manage to get that garter belt off without taking off her pants first, would you mind telling me?"

"I . . . I don't know," Christine said. "Maybe she got undressed and then . . . then felt chilly or something, and put the panties on again. Really, she could have . . ."

"Or maybe somebody put them on *for* her! Somebody who didn't know the first thing about dressing or undressing a woman!" He looked at her wildly and then nodded and then punched his fist into the open palm of his other hand. "Where are my shoes?" he said.

Too much has been said about the guilt complex of the American people. Too much has been said about the Puritan heritage, and a culture seemingly designed to encourage all sorts of anxiety. Hawes didn't know whether the average American male carried guilt around in him like a stone, nor did he much give a damn about the average American male on the night he went to make his arrest. He did know that a guilty criminal is an American who *is* carrying guilt in him like a stone, and he further knew he didn't have a chance in hell of cracking a case that was already in the Open File unless he made use of that guilt. There were probably a hundred easy explanations for why Irene Thayer was found dead with her panties on and her garter belt off. Christine had provided one at the drop of a hat, and a clever murderer could possibly

148

provide another dozen if pressed only slightly. So Hawes didn't go to the house in Riverhead with the idea of thrashing out the correct procedure for removing a woman's undergarments. He went there with a lie as big as the house itself, a lie designed to bring the guilt to the surface immediately. He went to that house to make an arrest, and everything in his manner indicated he knew all the facts of the case and wasn't ready to listen to any nonsense. As a start, he rapped on the door of the house with his drawn .38.

He waited in the darkness. He would wait another two minutes, and then he would shoot the lock off the door. He didn't have to wait nearly that long. He heard footsteps approaching the door, and then the door opened, and Amos Barlow said, "Yes?" and Hawes thrust the gun at him and said, "Get your hat, Mr. Barlow. It's all over."

"What?" Barlow said. A look of complete astonishment crossed his face. He stared out at Hawes with his eyes opened wide.

"You heard me. It's finished. We just got a lab report."

"What? What lab report? What are you talking about?"

"I'm talking about your fingerprints on the glass you washed and put in the kitchen cabinet," Hawes lied. "I'm talking about the murder of your own brother and Irene Thayer. Now get your goddamn hat because this has been a long day, and I'm tired, and I'm just liable to shoot and end it right here and now."

He waited in the darkness with the gun poised, waited with his heart pounding inside his chest because he didn't know whether or not Barlow would call his bluff. If he did call it, if he said he didn't know what Hawes was talking about, what glass? what kitchen cabinet? what prints? if he did that, Hawes knew there wasn't a chance in hell of ever cracking the case. It would rot in the Open File forever.

In a very soft voice, Barlow said, "I thought I'd washed it."

"You did," Hawes said quickly. "You missed a print near the bottom of the glass."

"I thought I'd been very careful," he said. "I went over the place very carefully." He shook his head. "Did you . . . have you known this very long?"

"The lab was backed up with work. We just got the report tonight."

"Because I thought . . . I thought when you were here the last time looking for the film, I thought that was the end of it. I thought you'd close the case after that."

"What *did* you do with the film, Mr. Barlow?"

"I burned it. I realized it had been a mistake, taking it like that, and I waited a long time before deciding to get rid of it. But . . . I wanted something of Tommy. Do you know? I wanted something to remind me of Tommy." He shook his head. "I burned it two days before you came looking for it. I thought that was the end of it, when you came around that time. I thought the case would be closed."

"Why'd you do it, Mr. Barlow?" Hawes asked. "Why'd you kill them?"

Barlow stared up at him for a moment, a slight man with a lopsided stance, a cane in his right hand. And for that moment, Hawes felt an enormous sympathy for him; he looked at Barlow standing in the doorway of the house he had bought with his brother and tried to understand what had pushed this man into doing murder.

"Why'd you do it?" he asked again.

And Barlow, staring at Hawes, and through Hawes, and past him to a night long ago in April, said simply, "The idea just came to me," and Hawes put the handcuffs onto his wrists.

The idea just came to me. You have to understand that I didn't go up there with the idea of killing them. I didn't even know Irene Thayer existed, you understand, so I couldn't have planned to kill them. You have to realize that. Tommy told me that morning that he had a surprise for me, and he gave me an address and told me to come there on my lunch hour. I go to lunch every day at twelve-thirty. I could hardly wait to know what Tommy's surprise was. I could hardly wait for lunch that day.

So at twelve-thirty I came down from my office and I took a cab uptown to the address he had given me. 1516 South Fifth Street. That was the address. Apartment 1A. That's where I went. I walked upstairs, and I rang the bell and Tommy opened the door with a big smile on his face, he was a happy-go-lucky person, you know, always laughing, and he asked me to come in, and then he took me into the living room, and the girl was there.

Irene.

Irene Thayer.

He looked at me and he said, "Irene, this is my brother, Amos," and then with the smile still on his face he said to me, "Amos, this is Irene Thayer,"

150

and I was reaching for her hand to shake hands with
her when he said, "We're getting married next month."

I couldn't believe him, do you know? I hadn't
even <u>heard</u> about this girl, and now he'd invited me
to this strange apartment on South Fifth and he'd
introduced her and told me he was going to marry her
next month, and all without ever having even told
me he was serious about anybody. I mean, I'm his
brother. He could have at least told me.

They . . . they had two bottles of whisky there.
Tommy said he had bought them to celebrate. He
poured out some whisky, and we drank to the coming
marriage, and all the while I was thinking why hadn't
he told me before this, why hadn't he told his own
brother? We're . . . we were very close, you know.
It was Tommy who took care of me after my mother and
father died, he was like a father to me, I swear it,
there was real love between us, real love. And
while we drank, while I was all the time wondering why
he hadn't told me about this Irene Thayer, they began
to explain that Irene was married and that she would
be leaving for Reno and that as soon as she got her
divorce Tommy was going to join her there and they
planned to spend their honeymoon out West, and then
maybe Tommy would take a job out there, he wasn't so
sure, but he had heard there were a great many
opportunities in California. He might, he said, try
to get something in the picture business. He was
always fooling around with film, you know, him and
this fellow who worked at his place with him.

So we drank, and I began to realize that not only
was he getting married to this strange girl I'd just
met, but also he was planning on moving out, maybe
living in California permanently, after we'd just
bought a house for ourselves, well not just that
minute, but we'd only been in the new house less than
a year, and here he was talking of leaving it, of
living in California, all the way on the other end of
the country. I began to feel a little sick, and I
excused myself and went into the bathroom, feeling
nauseated, sick to my stomach, you know, and I looked
in the medicine cabinet to see if there was some
Alka-Seltzer or something, anything to quiet my
stomach, and that was when I saw the sleeping pills,
and I guess that was when I got the idea.

I guess so, anyway. I'm not sure. I mean, I don't
think I knew then that I was going to turn on the gas
or anything, but I <u>did</u> know I was going to put the
pills in their drinks, maybe I thought they'd die <u>that</u>

way, do you know what I mean, from an overdose of
sleeping pills. When I came out, I had the bottle of
pills in my pocket. There were four pills in the
bottle. Tommy poured fresh drinks, and I went into
the kitchen with them, to put water in them, you know,
we were drinking Scotch and water, and that was when
I put the pills into their glasses, two pills in each
glass, I figured that would be enough to put them to
sleep, or maybe to kill them, I don't know what I
figured. The pills worked very fast. I was glad they
did because my lunch hour was almost over, and I've
never been late in all the time I've worked for
Anderson and Loeb, never late getting to work in the
morning, and not coming back from lunch, either. They
were both asleep in maybe fifteen minutes, and I
looked at them, and I realized they weren't dead, only
asleep, and I guess, yes, that must have been when,
yes, I guess that was when I decided that I would have
to kill them because, I don't know, because I didn't
want Tommy to marry this girl and go to live all the
way in California, yes, I suppose that was when I
decided to turn on the gas.

I carried them into the bedroom and put them on
the bed, and then I saw the typewriter on the stand
alongside the bed, and I typed up the note on the
machine and put it on the dresser. I don't know why I
misspelled the word "ourselves." I think it was
just a mistake I made, because I don't know how to
type, I just pecked the note out with two fingers, but
there wasn't any eraser in the room, and besides I
thought the mistake made the note look more genuine,
so I left it there. I took off Tommy's watch to hold
the note down on the dresser, and that was when I
got the idea of taking off their clothes. I guesss I
wanted to make it look as if this had been a love nest,
do you know, as if they had just done it, do you
know? I mean, before they turned on the gas. So I
took off all their clothes, and folded them on the
chairs, I tried to make it look the way I thought it
would look if they had really taken off their own
clothes before doing it. Then I went around the
apartment and wiped everything I could remember
touching, but I couldn't remember what I'd touched and
what I hadn't, so I just wiped everything, with my
handkerchief. I found the film in the living room
while I was wiping the things off in there. It had
Tommy's name on the can, and I remember meeting his
friend one time, and I remembered they'd made some
movies together, so I put the reel in my coat pocket.

152

Then I took the whisky bottles into the bedroom, and I opened the second one to make it look as if they'd been drinking a lot, and I spilled it out on the rug to make it look as if they'd got real drunk before turning on the gas, but I still hadn't turned it on, even though the idea was in my head all the time, I knew I was going to do it, but I still hadn't turned it on yet. While I was in the bedroom with the whisky bottles, I looked at the two of them on the bed, and it began bothering me, the two of them on the bed the way they were. I kept thinking about them all the while I was in the kitchen washing out the glasses. I washed and dried all three glasses, and I left two of them in the sink to make it look as if they'd been drinking alone together, and I put the third glass back in the cabinet where all the other glasses were. I thought I'd wiped them all clean. But I guess your lab has ways of finding out, it was silly of me to think they wouldn't find out, with their microscopes and all. But all the while I was washing the glasses, I kept thinking of them on the bed there, and it kept bothering me that they would be found undressed even though I wanted it to look like love. So I went back into the bedroom, and I put their underwear back on, Tommy's and the girl's. I would have put on her . . . her brassiere, but . . . I . . . I didn't know how. So I . . . I did what I could. Then I stood in the doorway and looked into the room for a minute to see if it still looked like love, and I decided that it did, and that was when I went into the kitchen and turned on the gas, and left the apartment.

When the stenographer delivered the typed confession, Amos Barlow signed it and went limping out of the room with a patrolman who took him downstairs to the detention cells where he would be kept overnight until his arraignment the next morning. They watched him as he limped out of the squadroom. They could hear the sound of his cane on the iron-runged steps leading to the downstairs level. They listened to it without a sense of triumph, without even a sense of completion.

"You fellows want some coffee?" Miscolo asked, standing just outside the door of the clerical office.

"No, thanks, none for me," Carella said.

"Cotton? Some tea?"

153

"Thanks, Alf. No."

The men were silent. The clock on the wall read ten minutes to one. Outside the grilled windows of the squadroom, a light, early morning rain had begun to fall.

Carella sighed heavily and put on his jacket. "I was just sitting here and wondering how many people commit murder on the spur of the moment, and get away with it. I was just wondering."

"Plenty," Hawes said.

Carella sighed again. "You got any brothers, Cotton?"

"No."

"Neither have I. How can a man kill his own brother?"

"He didn't want to lose him," Hawes said.

"He lost him," Carella answered flatly, and then he sighed again and said, "Come on, I'll buy you a beer. You want a beer?"

"All right," Hawes said.

They went down the corridor together. Outside the clerical office, they both stopped to say good night to Miscolo. As they came down the iron-runged steps to the first floor, Carella said, "What time are you coming in tomorrow?"

"I thought I'd get in a little early," Hawes said.

"Trying for a line on Petie?"

"He's still with us, you know."

"I know. Anyway, Bert thinks he's got a lead on that numbers bank. We may be hitting it tomorrow, and that'll shoot the whole damn afternoon. Be a good idea to get in early."

"Maybe we ought to skip the beer."

"I'd just as soon, if it's okay with you," Carella said.

It had begun raining harder by the time they came out into the street.